Welcome to the world of
St Piran's Hospital.

Next to the rugged shores of Penhally Bay
lies the picturesque Cornish town of St Piran,
where you'll find a bustling hospital famed
for the dedication, talent and passion
of its staff—on and off the wards!

Under the warmth of the Cornish sun
Italian doctors, heart surgeons, and
playboy princes discover that romance
blossoms in the most unlikely of places…

You'll also meet the devilishly handsome
Dr Josh O'Hara and the beautiful,
fragile Megan Phillips…and discover the
secret that tore these star-crossed lovers apart.

Turn the page to step into St Piran's—
where every drama has a dreamy doctor…
and a happy ending.

Dear Reader

St Piran's has been such a huge success that I was delighted to be invited to write the final book in the series. I was even more delighted when I saw my brief and realised that I had been given such a fantastic hero and heroine.

Tasha is a paediatric doctor, and she's bright, feisty, brave and bold. She's a woman who isn't afraid to stand up for what she believes is right— even if that means challenging those in authority. To protect her tiny patients she's risked her career, and her passionate determination to do the right thing has saved two lives but cost her her job. She's the sort of doctor I'd want fighting my corner if one of my children were sick—the sort of doctor who puts ethics before establishment. But even fiery Tasha has her insecurities, and when her big brother Josh arranges for her to nurse his friend Prince Alessandro this strong, opinionated doctor suddenly finds herself at her most vulnerable. Faced with the gorgeous, sexy Prince she fell crazily in love with as a teenager, suddenly she's not so brave and bold...

As well as writing Tasha and Alessandro's story, I was also allowed to develop the exciting, forbidden romance between Josh and Megan. There were so many dramatic twists and turns to their relationship that I was desperate to know how it ended. I hope you feel the same way, and enjoy exploring the developing relationship between these characters.

Love

Sarah x

ST PIRAN'S:
PRINCE ON THE
CHILDREN'S WARD

BY
SARAH MORGAN

First published in Great Britain 2011
by Mills & Boon, an imprint of Harlequin (UK) Limited.
Large Print edition 2011
Harlequin (UK) Limited, Eton House,
18-24 Paradise Road, Richmond, Surrey TW9 1SR

© Harlequin Books S.A. 2011

Special thanks and acknowledgement are given
to Sarah Morgan for her contribution to the
St Piran's Hospital series

ISBN: 978 0 263 21780 3

Harlequin (UK) policy is to use papers that are
natural, renewable and recyclable products and made
from wood grown in sustainable forests. The logging
and manufacturing process conform to the legal
environmental regulations of the country of origin.

Printed and bound in Great Britain
by CPI Antony Rowe, Chippenham, Wiltshire

Sarah Morgan is a British writer who regularly tops bestseller lists with her lively stories for both Mills & Boon® Medical™ Romance and Modern™ Romance.

As a child Sarah dreamed of being a writer, and although she took a few interesting detours on the way she is now living that dream. With her writing career she has successfully combined business with pleasure, and she firmly believes that reading romance is one of the most satisfying and fat-free escapist pleasures available. Her stories are unashamedly optimistic, and she is always pleased when she receives letters from readers saying that her books have helped them through hard times.

RT Book Reviews has described her writing as 'action-packed and sexy'. Her writing is widely acclaimed and she has been nominated twice for a Reviewer's Choice Award, shortlisted twice for the Romance Prize by the Romantic Novelists' Association, and most recently finalled for a RITA® Award by Romance Writers of America.

Sarah lives near London with her husband and two children, who innocently provide an endless supply of authentic dialogue. When she isn't writing or nagging about homework Sarah enjoys music, movies, and any activity that takes her outdoors.

Recent titles by the same author:

DR ZINETTI'S SNOWKISSED BRIDE
CHRISTMAS EVE: DOORSTEP DELIVERY
SNOWBOUND: MIRACLE MARRIAGE
THE GREEK BILLIONAIRE'S LOVE-CHILD
ITALIAN DOCTOR, SLEIGH-BELL BRIDE

ST PIRAN'S HOSPITAL
*Where every drama has a dreamy doctor…
and a happy ending.*

**Nick Tremayne and Kate Althorp
finally got their happy-ever-after in:**
ST PIRAN'S: THE WEDDING OF THE YEAR
by Caroline Anderson

**Dr Izzy Bailey was swept off her feet
by sexy Spaniard Diego Ramirez**
ST PIRAN'S: RESCUING PREGNANT CINDERELLA
by Carol Marinelli

**The arrival of Italian neurosurgeon Giovanni Corezzi
is guaranteed to make your heart beat faster**
ST PIRAN'S: ITALIAN SURGEON, FORBIDDEN BRIDE
by Margaret McDonagh

**Daredevil doc William MacNeil
unexpectedly discovered that he's a father in:**
ST PIRAN'S: DAREDEVIL, DOCTOR…AND DAD!
by Anne Fraser

The new heart surgeon had everyone's pulses racing in:
ST PIRAN'S: THE BROODING HEART SURGEON
by Alison Roberts

**Then fireman Tom Nicholson
stole Flora Loveday's heart in:**
ST PIRAN'S: THE FIREMAN AND NURSE LOVEDAY
by Kate Hardy

**Last month newborn twins brought a marriage miracle
for Brianna and Connor Taylor**
ST PIRAN'S: TINY MIRACLE TWINS
by Maggie Kingsley

**And finally this month
playboy Prince Alessandro Cavalieri comes to St Piran**
ST PIRAN'S: PRINCE ON THE CHILDREN'S WARD
by Sarah Morgan

CHAPTER ONE

TASHA rehearsed her speech as she walked through the busy emergency department towards the on-call room. Inside she was panicking, but she was determined not to let that show.

Hello, dear darling brother, I know you're not expecting me, but I thought I'd just drop in and see how you're doing. No, she couldn't say that. He'd know instantly that something was wrong.

You're looking gorgeous today. No, way too creepy, and anyway they usually exchanged insults so he'd definitely know something was up.

Josh, of all my brothers, you've always been my favourite. No. She didn't have favourites.

You're the best doctor in the world and I've always admired you. That one just might work. Her brother certainly was an excellent doctor. He'd been her inspiration. And her rock. When their father had walked out, leaving his four children and his fragile, exhausted wife, it had been Josh, the eldest, who had taken charge. Wild, handsome Josh, whose own marriage was now in a terrible state.

But at least he'd had the courage to get married, Tasha thought gloomily. She couldn't ever imagine herself doing anything that brave.

Was it because of their parents, she wondered, that all the O'Haras were so bad at relationships?

Since her last relationship disaster, she'd given up and concentrated on her career. A career couldn't break your heart—or so she'd thought until a few weeks ago.

Now she knew differently.

Terror gripped her

She'd messed everything up.

Hating the feeling of vulnerability, Tasha stopped outside the door. Fiercely independent, it stuck in her throat that she needed to ask her brother for help, but she swallowed her pride and knocked. She needed someone else's perspective on what had happened and the one person whose judgement she trusted was her older brother.

Seconds later the door was jerked open and Josh stood there, buttoning up his shirt. His hair was dishevelled and he was badly in need of a shave. Clearly he'd had a night with no sleep but what really caught her attention was the stupid grin on his face. A grin that faded the instant he saw her.

'Tasha?' Astonishment was replaced by shock and he cast a fleeting glance over his shoulder before pushing her back into the corridor and closing the door firmly behind him. 'What are you doing here?'

'What sort of greeting is that?' Badly in need of a hug, Tasha heard her voice thicken and the bruises of the last month ached and throbbed inside her. 'I'm your little sister. You're supposed to be pleased to see me.'

'I am, of course, but—Tash, it's seven-thirty in the morning.' Josh let out a breath and rubbed his hand over his face to wake himself up. His free hand. The one that wasn't holding the doorhandle tightly. 'I wasn't expecting— You took me by surprise, that's all. How did you know where I was?'

'I asked one of the nurses. Someone said they thought you were in the on-call room. What's wrong with you? You look ruffled.' It was the first time she'd seen her cool, confident brother anything other than immaculate. Tasha looked from him to the door that he was holding tightly shut. 'Did I wake you?'

'No. I— Yes, but it doesn't matter.'

'Busy night?'

'Sort of.' His gaze darted to the corridor and back to her. 'What are you *doing* here, Tasha?'

Because she was watching his face, she saw the fevered expression in her brother's eyes and the way the flush spread across his cheekbones. The signs pointed to one thing…

He had a woman in the room.

But why be so secretive about the whole thing? His marriage to Rebecca was over—there was no reason why he shouldn't have a relationship. Surely he wasn't embarrassed about her knowing he had a sex life? It was no secret that women found her brother irresistible.

Still, it was a relief to find an explanation for his weird behaviour and she was about to tease him unmercifully when she remembered that she couldn't afford to antagonise him.

Instead, she gave him a playful punch on the arm. 'I thought I'd just drop in and see you.'

'Before breakfast?'

'I'm an early riser.'

'You mean you're in trouble.' His dry tone reminded her that her brother knew her too well.

Tasha thought about everything that had happened over the last month. *Had she done the wrong thing?* 'Not trouble exactly,' she hedged.

'I just thought it was a long time since we'd had a good chat. Is there somewhere we can talk?' She glanced at the on-call room but he jerked his head towards the corridor.

'My office. Let's go.'

Feeling like a schoolgirl on detention, Tasha slunk after him through the department, aware of the curious stares of the staff. The main area was packed with patients, including a young girl lying on a trolley, holding her mother's hand. Noticing that the child was struggling to breathe, Tasha moved instinctively towards her just as a doctor swept up in a white coat. With a murmur of apology, Tasha moved to one side, reminding herself that this wasn't her patient. Or even her hospital. She didn't work here, did she?

She didn't work anywhere.

Her stomach lurched. Had she been impulsive and hasty? *Stupid?*

It was all very well having principles, but was there a point where you should just swallow them?

Trapped by sudden panic, she paused. The conversation drifted towards her. 'Her hay fever has suddenly made her asthma worse,' the mother was telling the young doctor. 'Her breathing has been terrible and her eyes and face are all puffy.'

Tasha gave the child a sympathetic smile, wishing she was the one taking the history and searching for the problem. The fact that her hands ached to reach for a stethoscope simply renewed her feeling that she might have done the wrong thing.

Medicine, she thought. She loved medicine. It was part of her. Not working in a hospital made her feel like a plant dragged up by its roots and thrown aside. Without her little patients to care for, she was wilting.

Biting her tongue to stop herself intervening, she followed her brother down the corridor but something about the child nagged at her brain. Puffy eyes. Hay fever? Frustrated with herself for not being able to switch off, she quickened her pace. It wasn't her business. This wasn't even her department. And anyway, what did she know? She was feeling so battered and bruised by the events of the past few weeks she didn't trust herself to pass opinion on anything, not even the adverse effects of a high pollen count. Feeling really dejected, she followed her brother into his office.

It was stacked with books and medical journals. In one corner was a desk with a computer and an overflowing tray of paper. Tasha noticed that the photograph of Rebecca had gone and she felt a stab of guilt that she hadn't asked how he was. Was she was turning into one of those awful people who only thought about themselves? 'How are you doing? How are things with Rebecca?'

'Cordial. Our separation is probably the first thing we've ever agreed on. It's all in the hands of the lawyers. Sit down.' Josh shifted a pile of medical journals from the chair to the floor but Tasha didn't feel like sitting down. She was filled with restless energy. The stability of her brother's life contrasted heavily with the instability of her own. She'd been sailing along nicely through life and now she'd capsized her boat and she had no idea where the tide was going to take her.

The lump in her throat came from nowhere and she swallowed hard.

Damn.

Not now.

As the only girl in a family of four older brothers, she'd learned that if you cried, you never heard the last of it.

Fighting the emotion, she walked to the window and opened it. 'I love Cornwall.' She closed her eyes and breathed deeply. 'I've lived in so many places since I became a doctor and yet this is still home. I can smell the sea. I can't wait to pick up my surfboard. I've been trapped in a city for too long.' The plaintive shriek of a seagull made her open her eyes and for a moment the memories threatened to choke her.

Home.

'So, what brings you banging on my door at this unearthly hour—what have you done?' Josh sounded distracted. 'Please tell me you haven't killed a patient.'

'No!' Outrage was sharp and hot, slicing through the last of her composure. 'Far from it. I *saved* a patient. Two patients, actually.' Tasha clenched her fists, horrified to realise just how badly she needed someone else to tell her she'd done the right thing. *That she hadn't blown her career on a childish whim.* 'I had an incident— sort of. You know when you just have a feeling about a patient? Perhaps you haven't actually had test results back from the lab, but sometimes you don't need tests to tell you what you already know. Well, I had one of my feelings—a really strong feeling. I know it wasn't exactly the way to go about things, but—'

'Tasha, I'm too tired to wade through hours of female waffle. Just tell me what you've done. Facts.'

'I'm not waffling. Medicine isn't always black

and white. You should know that.' Tasha's voice was fierce as she told him about the twins, the decisions she'd made and the drug she'd used.

Josh listened and questioned her. 'You didn't wait for the results of the blood cultures? And if it wasn't on the hospital-approved formulary—'

'They had it in stock for a different indication. You remember I went to the conference of the American Academy of Pediatrics last year? I told you about it when we met for supper that night. The data is *so* strong, Josh. We should be using it in Britain, but it's all money, money, money—'

'Welcome to the reality of health-care provision.'

'The drug is at least fifty per cent more effective than the one I was supposed to use.'

'And three hundred per cent more expensive.'

'Because it's good,' Tasha snapped, 'and research of that quality comes at a price.'

'Don't lecture me on the economics of drug development.'

'Then don't lecture me on wanting to do the best for my patients. Those babies would have died, Josh! If I'd waited for the results or used a different drug, they would have died.' In her head she saw their tiny bodies as they lay with the life draining out of them. She heard their mother's heartbreaking sobs and saw the father, white faced and stoical, trying to be a rock while his world fell apart. And she saw herself, facing the most difficult decision of her professional life. 'They lived.' She felt wrung out. Exhausted. But telling her brother had somehow made everything clearer. Whatever happened to her, whatever the future held, it had been worth the price. She didn't need anyone else to tell her that.

'The drug worked?'

'Like magic.' The scientist in her woke up and excitement fizzed through her veins. 'It could transform the management of neonatal sepsis.'

'Have you written it up for one of the journals?'

'I'm going to. I just need to find the time.' And now she had time, she thought gloomily. Oodles of it.

'But the hospital authorities didn't approve and now you're in trouble?'

'I didn't exactly follow protocol, that's true, but I'd do the same thing again in the same circumstances. Unfortunately, my boss didn't agree.' Tasha turned her head and stared out of the window. 'Which is why I resigned.' Saying the word made her heart plummet. It sounded so—final.

'You did what?' Josh sounded appalled. 'Please tell me you're kidding.'

'No. I resigned on principle.' The anger rose, as fresh and raw as it had been on that morning when she'd faced her boss after two nights without sleep. 'I said to him, *What sort of department are you running when your budget comes before a baby's life?*'

'And no doubt you went on to tell him what sort of department he was running. Tactful, Tasha.' Josh rubbed his hand over his jaw. 'So you questioned his professional judgement and dented his ego.'

'A man of his position shouldn't need to have his ego protected. He shouldn't be that pathetic.'

'Did you tell him that as well?'

'I told him the truth.'

Josh winced. 'So…I'm assuming, given that he was the sort of guy to protect his ego, that he didn't take it well?'

'He's the sort of person who would stand and watch someone drown if health and safety hadn't approved a procedure for saving them. He said the manufacturer did not present a sufficiently robust economic analysis.' Tasha felt the emotion rush down on her and forced herself to breathe. 'So then I asked him if he was going to be the one who told the parents they'd lost both their babies because some idiot in a suit sitting behind his desk had crunched the numbers and didn't think their children's lives were worth the money.'

Josh closed his eyes briefly. 'Tasha—'

'Sorry.' The lump in her throat was back and this time it wasn't going anywhere. 'I *know* I should have been unemotional about the whole thing but I just can't be. Honestly, I'm steaming mad.'

'You don't say? Are you about to cry on me?'

'No, absolutely not.'

'The only time I've ever seen you cry was when Cheapskate died.'

They shared a look. Cheapskate had been the dog their mother had bought after their father had walked out. Tasha remembered hugging his warm body and feeling his tail thumping against her leg. She remembered thinking, *Don't ever leave me,* and then being devastated when he'd done just that.

'He was a great dog.'

'He was a lunatic.' But Josh's eyes were gentle. 'Tell me about those babies you saved. Are they still doing well?'

'Discharged home. You should have seen it, Josh. You know what it's like, trying to calculate these paediatric doses—they never have trial data in the right age of child, but this...' She smiled, the doctor in her triumphant. 'It's why I trained. To push boundaries. To save a life.'

'And you saved two.'

'And lost my job.'

'You shouldn't have resigned.'

It was a question she'd asked herself over and over again. 'I couldn't work with the man a moment longer. He was the sort who thought women should be nurses, not doctors. Basically he's a—a—' She bit off the word and Josh gave a faint smile.

'I get the picture. Has it occurred to you that you might be too idealistic, Tasha?'

'No. Not too idealistic.' The conviction came from deep inside her. 'Isn't that why we're doctors? So that we can push things forward? If we all did what doctors have always done and no more, we wouldn't have progress.'

'There are systems—'

'And what if those systems are wrong? I can't work for someone like that. Sooner or later I would have had to inject him with something seriously toxic...' Tasha gave a cheeky smile '...but first I would, of course, have made sure it was approved by the formulary committee.'

'You're incorrigible.'

'No, I'm a doctor. I can accept that there are some patients I can't help. What I *can't* accept is that there are some patients I'm not allowed to help because someone has decided the treatment is too expensive! I mean, who decides what's important?' Tasha paced across his office, her head swirling with the same arguments that had tormented her for weeks. 'I told him that if the chief executive took a pay cut we'd be able to easily fund this drug for the few babies likely to need it.'

'I'm beginning to see why you felt the need to resign.'

'Well, what would you have done?'

'I have no idea.' Her brother spread his hands. 'It's impossible to say if you're not in that situation. Why didn't you wait for the blood cultures? Or use the first-line choice?'

'Because the twins were getting sicker by the minute and I felt that time was crucial. If we'd waited for that one drug, only for it to fail… My instincts were shrieking at me, Josh. And even while I was running tests, my consultant was telling me it wasn't sepsis and that the twins were suffering from something non-specific caused by the stress of delivery.' And she'd spun it around in her head, over and over again, looking for answers. 'Sometimes you see a patient and you're going through the usual and it all seems fine, except you know it isn't fine because something in here...' she tapped her head '...something in here is sending you warnings loud and clear.'

'You can't practise medicine based on emotion.'

'I'm not talking about emotion. I'm talking about instinct. I tell you, Josh, I *know* when a child isn't well. Don't ask me how.' She held up her hand to silence him. 'I just know. And I was right with the twins. But apparently that didn't matter to Mr Tick-All-The-Boxes Consultant. He has to play things by the book and if the book is wrong, tough. Which is a lame way to practise medicine.'

'And no doubt you told him that, too?'

'Of course. By the time he'd had all his evidence, he would have had two dead bodies. And he was angry with me because I saved their lives. He could have had a lawsuit on his hands, but did he thank me?' The injustice of it was like a sharp knife in her side, digging, twisting. 'Haven't you ever used instinct when you treat a patient?'

'If by instinct you mean clinical judgement, then, yes, of course, but, Tasha—'

'Wait a minute.' Tasha interrupted him, her brain working and her eyes wide. 'That little girl—'

'What little girl?'

'The one waiting to be seen in the main area. I heard the mother say that hay fever was making her asthma worse, but her eyelids were swollen and her face was puffy. I thought at the time that something wasn't right—just didn't seem like allergy to me—and—'

'That little girl is not your patient, Tasha.'

'She was wheezing.'

'As she would if she had asthma.'

'As she would if she had left-sided venous congestion. I knew there was something about her that bothered me.' Tasha picked up his phone and thrust it at him. 'Call the doctor in charge of her, Josh. Tell her to do the tests. Maybe she will anyway, but maybe she won't. In my opinion, that child has an underlying heart condition. Undiagnosed congenital anomaly? She needs an ECG and an echo.'

'Tasha—'

'Just do it, Josh. Please. If I'm wrong, I'll give up and get a job in a garden centre.'

With a sigh, Josh picked up his phone and called the doctor responsible for seeing the child.

While he talked, Tasha stood staring out of the window, wishing she didn't always get so upset about everything. Why couldn't she be emotionally detached, like so many of her colleagues? Why couldn't she just switch off and do the job?

'She's going to do a full examination, although she thinks it's asthma and allergy combined. We'll see. And now you need to relax.' Josh's voice was soft. 'You're in a state, Tasha.'

'I'm fine.' It was a lie. She'd desperately wanted a hug but was afraid that if someone touched her she'd start crying and never stop. 'But I do find myself with a lot of free time on my hands. I thought...' She hesitated, *hating* having to crawl to her brother. 'You're important. Can you pull a few strings here? Get me a job? The paediatric department has a good reputation.'

'Tasha—'

'Paediatrics is my life. My career. I'm good, Josh. I'm good at what I do.'

'I'm not debating that, but—'

'Yes, you are. You're worrying I'll mess things up for you here.'

'That isn't true.' Josh stood up and walked over to her. 'Calm down, will you? You're totally stressed out. Maybe what you need is a break from hospitals for a while.'

'What I need is a *job*. I love working with kids. I love being a doctor. And then there's the practical side. I was living in a hospital flat so now I'm homeless as well as jobless.' Tasha felt as though she had an enormous mountain to climb. 'Resigning seemed like the only option at the time. Now I realise why more people don't resign on principle. It's too expensive.'

'I can't pull strings to get you a job at the hospital, Tasha. Not at the moment. We've spent a fortune opening a new paediatric burns unit. There's a head-count freeze.'

'Oh.' Her stomach swooped and fell as another door slammed shut in her face. 'No worries. I'll sort something out.' She tried to subdue the niggling worry that her last consultant wouldn't give her a decent reference. 'Sorry, I shouldn't have asked you. I shouldn't have just shown up here.' *The list of things she shouldn't have done was growing.*

'I'm glad you did. It's been too long since I saw you. All you've done for the past three years is work. Since things ended with Hugo, in fact.'

Hugo? Shrinking, Tasha wondered why her brother had chosen that particular moment to bring up her disastrous love life. Could the day get any worse? 'I love my work.' *Why was he looking at her like that?* 'What's wrong with loving my work?'

'No need to get defensive. Maybe it's time to take a break. Rediscover a social life.'

'Social life? What's that?'

'It's part of work-life balance. You were going to get married once.'

The reminder scraped like sandpaper over sensitive skin. 'A moment of madness.' Tasha spoke through her teeth. 'Do you mind if we don't talk about it? Just thinking about Hugo makes me want to put my fist through something and at the moment I can't afford to pay for the damage. Anyway, you're a fine one to talk. You're a total workaholic.' *But he'd spent the night with a woman.*

Tasha wondered if he'd confide in her, but Josh was flicking through some papers on his desk.

'How flexible are you?'

'I can touch my toes and do a back flip.' Her joke earned her an ironic glance.

'The job,' he drawled. 'How would you feel about a break from paediatrics?'

'I love paediatrics, but…' But she was desperate. She needed something. Not just for the money but to stop herself thinking and going slowly mad. She needed to be active. 'What do you have in mind?'

'I happen to know a man in desperate need of twenty-four-hour nursing care for the next month or so. He's asked me to sort something out for him.'

Tasha instinctively recoiled. 'You want me to give bed baths to some dirty old man who's going to pinch my bottom?' She frowned at the laughter in her brother's eyes. 'What's so funny about that? You have a sick sense of humour.'

'What if I tell you the guy in question happens to be seriously rich.'

'Who cares?' Tasha thrust her hands into the back pockets of her jeans, wondering what Josh was finding so funny. Her brother was clearly enjoying a joke at her expense and she felt a flash of irritation that he could laugh when she was in such a mess. 'What's the relevance of his financial status? You think I'll nurse him, he'll fall in love and marry me, then I'll kill him off and inherit his millions? When you suggested a job change, I didn't realise you were talking about a sugar daddy.'

'He's too young to be your sugar daddy.'

'And I'm not interested in marriage. I'm a cold-hearted career-woman, remember? I'm dedicating my life to my patients. So far my longest and most successful relationship has been with my stethoscope.'

'This guy isn't interested in marriage either, so you'll make a good pair. Strictly speaking, he should be in hospital for at least another week but he's creating hell so they're happy to discharge him providing he arranges professional help. He needs someone medical to deliver quality care at home and he's willing to pay premium rates.' He named a figure that made Tasha's jaw drop.

'He obviously has more money than sense. What's the catch?'

'The catch is that he's an athletic, super-fit guy who isn't used to being stuck in bed. As a result his temper is somewhat volatile and he's terrifying everyone who comes within a metre of him. But I'm sure you'll cope with that. I'm guessing it will take you about—oh—five minutes before you point out his shortcomings.'

'As jobs go it doesn't sound appealing...' But it was a job. And it was just for a couple of weeks. 'I suppose it would give me something to do while I look for a more progressive paediatric department. A place where the patient takes priority over paperwork and protocol.' Tasha frowned as she weighed up the pros and cons. 'So basically I have to help Mr Grumpy Guy with his physio, say *There, there* when he's cranky, feed him antibiotics and check he's not weight bearing. Anything else I need to know? Like his name?'

Josh smiled. 'His name, little sister, is Alessandro Cavalieri.'

Tasha felt the strength drain from her legs. Her heart pounded with a rhythm that would have concerned her had she not been too busy staring at her brother. 'Alessandro? *The* Alessandro?'

'The very same. His Royal Highness.'

She hadn't thought it was possible for the whole body to blush. Suddenly she was a teenager again and sobbing her heart out. 'The answer is no.' The words stumbled out of her mouth, disjointed, shaky. 'No! And don't look at me like that.'

'I thought you'd jump at the chance. You were crazy about him. He was all you ever talked about—Alessandro, Alessandro, Alessandro.' Josh mimicked her tone and Tasha felt the flush of mortification spread from her neck to her ears.

'I was seventeen,' she snapped. 'It may have escaped your notice but I've grown up since then.' But not enough. Not enough to be cool and detached. Not Alessandro. *No, no, no.* The humiliation crawled over her skin.

'I know you've grown up. That's why I'm offering you the job. If you still felt the same way you felt about him back then, you wouldn't be safe.' Josh's eyes teased her. 'Oh, boy, were you dangerous. Teenage hormones on legs. You threw yourself at him. Being royalty, he travelled everywhere with an armed guard but the person he really needed protection from was you. Every time he turned round, there you were in another minuscule bikini. I seem to remember he told you to come back when you'd grown a chest.'

Tasha relived humiliation and discovered it was no better the second time around. Dying inside, she folded her arms and gave her brother a mocking smile. 'Laugh it up, why don't you?'

'My little sister and the prince. You used to scribble his name all over your school books. I particularly liked the *Princess Tasha* you carved on the apple tree in the garden, although the heart was a weird shape.' Josh was clearly enjoying himself hugely and Tasha tapped her foot on the floor, irritated on the outside and squirming on the inside as she remembered those horrible, hideous months.

She'd been a little girl with very big dreams. And when those dreams had burst... 'Have you quite finished?'

'For now. Good job you were a late developer or he might have taken you up on your offer. Alessandro has always had a wicked reputation with women.'

And her brother clearly had no idea just how well deserved that reputation was, Tasha thought desperately, trying to block out images she just couldn't face.

Josh was still smiling. 'Anyway, he's been nagging me to find him someone to nurse him but it's been a nightmare because of the security clearance. And I have to be careful who I give him because if they're pretty he'll seduce them. It's unbelievably complicated. You have no idea how much red tape we're trying to cut through. If we wait for the palace to approve someone, the guy will be in hospital for at least six months and that can't happen because the press are disrupting the place.'

'Why is security a problem?'

'He's the crown prince. Don't you watch the news? His older brother was killed in an accident. All very tragic.' Josh rummaged through the papers on his desk and pulled out a newspaper. 'Here. Your teenage crush is now officially Europe's most eligible bachelor.'

Tasha snatched the newspaper from him.

Her head was filled with unsettling images of Alessandro playing in the garden with her brothers. *Alessandro stripped to the waist, a sheen of sweat on his bronzed chest as he kicked a ball into the goal with lethal accuracy.* 'I read about his brother. It was completely awful.' She tried to imagine bad boy Alessandro as Crown Prince. Nothing about the way he'd treated her had been princely. 'He was the black sheep of the family.'

'Alessandro always had a difficult relationship with his parents but he was close to his brother. It's been hard for him. And he's now heir to a throne he doesn't really want. He prefers his freedom.'

Freedom to break hearts all over the world. 'I can't imagine Alessandro in a position of responsibility.' And that was the attraction. Restless, edgy, a danger-seeker. The devil in him had drawn her.

'He wasn't given any choice. It's a matter of succession. He's the heir, whether he likes it or not. So what do you think? I'd say it's the perfect job for you.' Josh was looking pleased with himself. 'You idolised him.'

'I did not idolise him. And the last thing I want to do is act as nurse to Alessandro Cavalieri,'

she snapped. 'He's arrogant, full of himself...'
Super-bright, scorching hot and sexy as hell.

He'd—and she'd—

Oh, God.

Feeling the blood rush into her cheeks, Tasha turned to look out of the window. She couldn't face him.

Sexual awareness shot through her, as unexpected as it was unwelcome. The man wasn't even in the room, she thought angrily, so why did she feel hot all over?

It was just her memory playing tricks.

What you found sexy at seventeen just made you angry at twenty-eight.

This was the man who had destroyed her dreams. He could have treated her kindly and let her down gently, but instead he'd been brutal. Cruel.

She should thank him, Tasha thought numbly. He'd screwed up her confidence and her relationships with men, but he'd done wonders for her career. When she'd finally emerged from under the rubble of her fantasies she'd given up on relationships and focused on her studies. Instead of parties, she'd spent her evenings with books. And her family hadn't questioned it. Her brothers had just been relieved that wild Tasha had finally settled down to study. They had no idea what had happened that night.

Thank goodness.

Josh would have killed him.

Her brother was idly flicking through correspondence, apparently unaware of her trauma. 'He was pretty arrogant, I suppose…' Josh signed a letter. 'But that was hardly surprising. When we were at university, women couldn't leave him alone.'

Tasha stood stiff as a board. 'Really?'

'You were crazy about him.' Josh dropped the letter in his in tray. 'Are you embarrassed to face him again?'

'No! Of course not! I just—have better things to do with my time, that's all. I'm a paediatrician. I need a job in paediatrics. I need to think of my CV.'

'Because it's just that it occurred to me that you did flirt with him a lot.'

I want it to be you, Alessandro. I want you to be the first.

Tasha felt as though she'd been plunged head first into a furnace. 'I was a teenage girl. I flirted with everyone.' Why was she reacting like this when it had happened almost ten years ago? *Get over it, Tasha.*

But humiliation wasn't so easily forgotten. Neither was Alessandro, which was crazy because she probably wouldn't even find him attractive any more. It had just been the whole prince thing and her impressionable, romantic teenage brain.

She knew better now.

Tasha leaned against the wall, forcing herself to breathe slowly. *Unfinished business*, she thought. He'd walked away and left her wounded. She'd never had the opportunity to defend herself, to tell him how much he'd hurt her.

Anger flashed through her, sharp and bright.

There was no way she could nurse him through a broken ankle. She was more likely to break the other one for him.

Tasha opened her mouth to turn her brother down and then a thought flitted into her brain. Shocked, she shook her head. *No. She couldn't do that.* It would be juvenile. Shallow. It would be…

Fun?

Satisfying?

It would teach him a lesson.

'This nursing job…' Her lips moved and she heard herself speaking. 'Does it involve moving in with him?'

'Yes, of course. He needs someone there day and night for a month or so. Maybe a bit longer.'

Day and night.

That was plenty of time to drive a man out of his mind.

To make him sorry.

She'd show him that he no longer had any effect on her and at the same time she'd finally purge him from her mind. The spectacular man in her head was the product of a teenage fantasy. Living with the reality would cure her of that once and for all. And it would give her a chance to restore her dignity.

Josh put his pen down slowly. 'You're thinking about it? A moment ago you were telling me he was arrogant and full of himself.'

'He was young. He's probably changed.' She didn't believe it for a minute. A man like Alessandro would never change. Looks, wealth and influence were welded together. 'It would be great to see him again. I'd like to help him.' Tasha tapped her foot on the floor as she considered the various forms that 'help' could take.

'You're sure you won't find it awkward? You were crazy about him.'

'Awkward? Gosh, no.' She told herself that whatever awkwardness she was going to feel would be eclipsed by his. And she'd be so dignified and mature about the whole thing, that would make him feel even worse. The plan grew in her head. 'I have to warn you, I'm not much of a nurse, Josh. I'm good with kids but moaning adults with man-flu drive me up the wall. I just want to tell them to pull themselves together.'

'It isn't man-flu. His ankle shattered and so far he's been back to Theatre four times. On top of that he has a couple of broken ribs and countless bruises.'

'So you're saying he's pretty much helpless?'

Better and better...

'Completely helpless. That's why it's important that we find the right person. He doesn't want to find himself trapped with someone who doesn't understand him.'

'Right. Well, that's good because I do understand him.' *She understood him perfectly.* He was a rich, handsome playboy who treated women like flashy accessories. His idea of permanency was two dates.

'It's important that whoever looks after him knows what he needs.'

Tasha looked sympathetic. 'I know *exactly* what he needs.' A wake-up call. A lesson in how to treat women properly. He was used to fawning women treating him with deference. And she needed to finally prove to herself that Alessandro Cavalieri was well and truly in her past. 'I'm very good at persuading patients to take their medicine, so I think I'm just the woman for the job.'

'I'm sure you are. You have good instincts and you're not scared of him. The staff here are intimidated by his status and afraid to tell him what he needs to do. He's walking all over them.'

'That can't be good for his broken ankle,' Tasha said lightly. 'Don't worry. I won't let him walk over me.' *Not this time.* This time she was going to be the one doing the walking.

She looked down at her trainers and wished she was wearing heels.

Josh was watching her. 'You're not going to fall for him again, are you?'

Tasha's laugh was genuine. 'Absolutely no chance of that.' She wasn't that stupid, was she? 'The only thing on my mind is my next job.'

'OK. Good—so you'll do it? Nag him about his physio and make sure he doesn't sneak women into his bed when he's supposed to be resting? Take care of him? That's great. Why don't you pop and see him right now? He's in a private room. I can give you directions.'

Right now?

Tasha's smile faltered. Her heart trebled its rhythm. No, not right now. She'd just lost her job. Well, not exactly *lost* it as such—she'd thrown it away. The last thing she needed was to heap on the humiliation. Facing Alessandro took serious preparation. She needed to get her head together. She needed to look her best.

Aware that Josh was looking at her, Tasha breathed slowly and tried to slow her pulse rate. If she said no, her brother would ask questions. And the longer she waited, the more the antici-pation would eat into her. And the advantage of doing it right away was that Alessandro wasn't forewarned. He wasn't expecting to see her.

Tasha strolled to the mirror in the corner of the office and stared at her reflection. Green eyes stared back at her. Green eyes that showed lack of sleep and stress. Doctor's eyes.

Apart from the shadows and the obvious ex-haustion, she didn't look that bad, did she?

Mouth too big, she thought. Freckles. Dark hair that twisted and curled over her shoulders. All wrong. As a teenager, she'd been horribly con-scious of her gypsy looks. She'd envied the girls with sleek blonde hair and china-blue eyes.

Insecurity crawled through her belly and she glared at her reflection, refusing to allow herself to think like that. At least she had a brain, which was more than could be said for most of Alessandro's women.

But there was no doubt that there was work to be done before she faced her past. Alessandro Cavalieri spent his time with the most beautiful women in the world. Facing him with confidence required more than an emergency repair job, but it would have to do.

With a sense of purpose, Tasha pulled her make-up case out of her bag.

'Poor Alessandro.' She darkened her lashes and added blusher to her cheeks. Not much. Just enough to help the 'natural' look. 'He must be going crazy, stuck in bed. You're right. What he needs is personal attention.'

And she was going to give him personal attention.

By the time she'd finished with him, a shattered ankle was going to be the least of his worries.

She was going to make him writhe with guilt for crushing her dreams so brutally. It was time he realised that women had feelings.

Josh was watching her in bemusement. 'Why are you putting on make-up?'

'Because I care how I look and because I want to look professional.' Staring into her bag, she selected a subtle gloss lipstick. 'Last time we met, I was a teenager. That's how he's going to remember me. I need to look like an adult—like someone capable of taking care of him.'

'You look very happy all of a sudden for someone who has just lost their job. A few moments ago I thought you were going to cry.'

'Me? Cry? Don't be ridiculous. Don't worry, Josh. I'll take good care of your friend.' Tasha tugged at the clip and her hair tumbled long and loose around her shoulders. Smiling to herself, she gave her head a shake. 'I'll take *extremely* good care of him.'

Alessandro Cavalieri had taken her fragile teenage heart and ground it under his feet.

Payback time, she thought as she added the high-shine gloss to her lips.

It was going to be her pleasure to give him exactly what he deserved.

And maybe, just maybe, once he'd given her a big, fat grovelling apology, she'd be able to put the whole episode behind her.

CHAPTER TWO

'YOUR Highness, you *can't* use your phone in the hospital.'

Alessandro turned frustrated dark eyes onto the nervous nurse, his temper reaching combustion point. 'Then get me out of hospital,' he said silkily, and watched as she bit her lip nervously.

'I'm really sorry but I don't have the authority to do that. You have an infection, Your Highness, and—'

'Stop calling me Your Highness.' The snap of the words was accompanied by a rush of guilt. *She was just a kid.* It wasn't her fault that he wanted the rank and title about as much as he wanted a badly smashed ankle and bruised ribs. 'I apologise,' he growled. 'Being stuck in here hasn't done much for my mood. I'm used to being active.' And lying in bed gave him too much time to think about things he spent his life trying to forget.

The darkness licked at the edges of his mind

threatening to engulf him. With a huge effort of will, he pushed it back.

Not now.

The nurse stood rigid, clearly overawed by her royal patient. 'The Chief Executive of the hospital called while you were with the consultant and asked me to tell you that he's increased security so that there's no repeat of yesterday's fiasco—he apologised profusely, Your Highness. We have no idea how that journalist managed to climb up the drainpipe to your room.' She all but curt-seyed but this time Alessandro kept his temper on a tight leash. It was obvious that she wasn't going to be able to behave naturally with him, and he'd encountered that all too often in his life to be surprised. No one behaved naturally with him. Everyone had an agenda.

'I'm used to journalists climbing drainpipes and crawling through the windows. It's a fact of life.' He reached for a glass of water, gritting his teeth against the agonising pain that shot through his body.

'Let me help you, sir.'

'I can manage.' Alessandro growled the words just as his shaking hand deposited most of the water over his chest. He switched to Italian, his native tongue, and swore long and fluently while the flustered nurse quietly removed the glass from his white fingers, refilled it and handed it to him.

She stared at his T-shirt, now clinging to his chest. 'Do you want me to—?'

'No. I'm fine.'

Dragging her eyes away from his muscles, the girl swallowed. 'Your senior adviser called, sir. He wanted you to call him urgently.'

Alessandro leaned his head back against the pillow and suppressed the urge to laugh out loud. That was the one good thing about this mess— his advisers were climbing the walls. The wicked side of him revelled in the chaos his accident had caused. 'I can't call him,' he drawled. 'You've just told me I'm not allowed to use my phone.'

'There's a phone by your bed, sir—Your Highness.'

For God's sake— 'You can call me Alessandro. And I think we've both just established that I can't reach anything that's by my bed.'

'There were a few other calls, Your Highness.' She gave him a nervous glance. 'Five journalists and four—er—women. None of them left their names. And Her Highness Princess Eleanor called when you were in the bathroom. She said not to bother calling her back but she left you a message.'

'Which was?'

'She saw on the news that the hospital is besieged by journalists and she asked that you be discreet about what you say to them.'

Alessandro gave a humourless smile.

The dull ache inside him turned into a dark black hole that threatened to suck him down.

So his mother had finally called.

Not when his accident had been announced as a newsflash and no one had known his condition. Not out of concern when he'd been rushed into Theatre for emergency surgery. Not to ask how he was or send love. No, his mother had called because she was worried about his image. Or rather she was worried about *her* image.

You have to think about how you present yourself, Alessandro. It affects all of us.

Wiping the cold, disapproving tone from his head, Alessandro sought distraction. The nurse was pretty, he realised, and he hadn't even noticed. Which said a great deal about his current state of mind. He had a wicked impulse to drag her to the window and kiss her senseless in front of the crowd of hopeful photographers.

But that wouldn't be fair on the girl.

Or on Miranda.

Thinking of Miranda was enough to kill his mood.

He was going to have to make a decision. They couldn't go on like this any longer. It wasn't fair on either of them.

'I don't suppose I can bribe you to smuggle me out of here?' He tried to look as non-threatening as possible. 'I own a home up the coast. Incredible views from the master bedroom.'

The nurse flushed scarlet and her eyes met his. He saw the excitement there and the way her lips parted as she caught her breath. Unfortunately he could also read her mind, which was busy spinning dreams ending with 'nurse marries Prince'.

Thinking of his parents' dutiful, entirely loveless marriage, he felt suddenly cold.

He had no idea why marriage was the ultimate goal for so many people. To him it seemed like the road to hell. He'd rather be trampled by a whole herd of horses than commit to one woman for the rest of his life. Especially a woman whose only interest in him was the fact he had royal blood.

'You understand that this is a purely indecent proposal.' He shifted his leg, but it did nothing to ease the pain. 'My house has amazing sea views from every room and a hot tub on the deck. You can scrub my back and give me a private physio session.'

'This is Cornwall.' A crisp female voice came from the doorway. 'If she uses the hot tub in April, she'll catch pneumonia. Hello, Alessandro. You look as though you're in a filthy mood. Hope I'm not supposed to bow or curtsey.'

It was a voice he hadn't heard for more than a decade, but the recognition was immediate and powerful. His body tightened in a reaction so basic, so elemental that he was relieved that he was confined to bed, with all the privacy that afforded. Temptation, he thought, wasn't something a man easily forgot. And Natasha O'Hara had been temptation on legs. A girl, desperate to become a woman. At seventeen, she'd tried everything to get him to notice her.

And he'd noticed.

Oh, yes, he'd noticed.

Remembering, Alessandro felt his muscles tighten. Sweat dampened his brow. He wasn't sure whether the pain in his chest was due to fractured ribs or guilt.

He'd treated her badly.

She strolled into the room with a confidence that told him the awkward teenager was long gone. There was no sign of the stiff formality that everyone else displayed around him. She didn't blush, call him 'Your Highness', or look as though she was about to bow and scrape at his feet. Her gaze was direct and challenging and he would have laughed with relief if it hadn't been for the uncomfortable feeling deep inside him. Tasha had always shown guts and intelligence. If someone had told her to bow or curtsey, her response would have been to ask why. One of the reasons he'd loved spending time with her was because she'd treated him as a normal human being.

And in return he'd broken her heart.

He shifted uncomfortably in the bed, but the guilt stayed with him.

Was she the sort of woman who bore grudges? Not for a moment did he think she would have forgotten that summer any more than he had.

'Are you going to pretend you don't recognise me?' Her tone was light and friendly and if she was bearing a grudge there was no sign of it.

Alessandro relaxed slightly. Maybe the guilt was misplaced. She'd been very young, he reasoned. He'd probably barely featured on her adolescent landscape. Everything healed quickly in childhood—broken bones and broken hearts.

Still watching him, she paused beside the bed. Her top was a vivid scarlet and she wore it tucked into skinny jeans, her dark hair tumbling down her back in snaky black curls. She looked like a cross between a gypsy and a flamenco dancer and Alessandro felt his mouth dry and his body harden in an all-male reaction.

The wild child had grown up.

'You've spilt water on your T-shirt.' She eyed his damp chest and he felt something stir inside him.

'It isn't easy manoeuvring with a broken ankle and two broken ribs.'

'Poor Alessandro.' Her voice poured over him like honey, soft and sympathetic. 'So that's why you're so cranky. It must be awful to feel so help-less.'

Pain gnawed at his temper, fraying his control. He'd kept his mind off the pain by thinking of ways to get himself out of the hospital, but her presence disturbed his focus. And the way she was looking at him felt wrong. He would have expected her to be angry with him or, if not angry, then at least a little shy? Or maybe embarrassed. After all, he'd— Alessandro moved awkwardly and pain rocketed through him. 'What are you doing here?' He ruthlessly ignored the pain. 'Josh mentioned that you worked at a hospital miles away.'

'Not any more. I'm…' she paused and then smiled '…in between jobs.'

Their eyes met and held and Alessandro wondered what the hell he'd done to deserve this extra punishment. 'You're looking good, Natasha.' *Too good,* he thought, noticing in that single reluctant glance that her body had fulfilled its teenage promise. As a girl, she'd been teenage temptation. As a woman, Natasha O'Hara was a vision of glorious curves that made a man think of nothing but wild sex. And thinking of wild sex made him ache in the only place that wasn't already aching, so he looked away from those smooth arms, tried to block out the image of those slender limbs and told himself that the last glossy mouth he'd kissed had led to nothing but trouble.

'Thanks, Nurse…er…' She squinted at the name badge. 'Carpenter. You've taken enough abuse from this patient for one day. I'll take it from here.'

Nurse Carpenter's face fell. 'But I've just come on duty and His Highness needs—'

'I know exactly what His Highness needs.' The words were a polite but firm dismissal and Alessandro tried to remember whether she'd had that air of command as a teenager. No, definitely not. She'd been full of wide-eyed, barely repressed excitement and optimism. 'Hopeless romantic' hadn't begun to describe her.

The nurse gave Alessandro a final wistful look and melted away.

Tasha closed the door firmly, leaving the two of them enclosed in the private room. 'Yes, Your Highness, no, Your Highness—it must drive you crazy. Or do you like your women servile?'

She was such a contrast to all the other people he'd come into contact with since he'd crashed into the mud on the polo field that Alessandro found himself laughing for the first time in weeks. 'Definitely not servile.'

'Good, because if I have to call you Your Highness every two minutes, this is never going to work.'

Alessandro watched as she strolled across the room. Something about the way she was looking at him made him uneasy. Or maybe it was just the guilt, he thought. It was definitely there, shimmering underneath the surface. 'What are you talking about?'

'You have to stop eating the nurses for breakfast, Alessandro. They're all terrified of you.'

'I'm a pussy cat.'

Her mouth flickered. 'Right.'

'Maybe I'm a little cranky, but I'm not good at lying in bed, doing nothing.'

'Then you'd better get used to it.' Her gaze was frank and direct. 'I looked at your X-rays. You won't be walking on that ankle for a while. You've made a mess of your bones.'

'Not me. The horse.' But it had been his fault and the knowledge gnawed at him. He'd been distracted. To take his mind off that, he studied her closely. *Was she taller or was it the way she held herself?* There was a confidence about her that hadn't been there a decade before. A knowledge of herself as a woman. It showed itself in the way her hips swayed when she walked and the hint of cleavage revealed by the neck of her casual top. Trapped and immobile, unaccustomed to feeling helpless in any situation, Alessandro set his teeth and tried to think cold thoughts. 'What are you doing here, Tasha?' He hadn't seen her since that night—the night when he'd left her sobbing, her make-up streaked over her beautiful face.

He pushed the memory aside, trying to lose it in the darkness of everything else he was trying to forget.

'Rumour is you're looking for a nurse so you can escape from this place.'

'In this case rumour is correct.' But he was starting to wonder whether being trapped at home with a star-struck nurse who called him Your Highness every two minutes might not be just as irritating as being in hospital.

'I can't imagine who would want the job. As temperaments go, yours is pretty volatile.'

'Once I'm out of here my temper will be just fine. Josh promised to find me a nurse by the end of the day. Do you know if he's had any luck?'

'Depends on your definition of luck.' She picked up the phone that he'd slung on the bedcover. 'You shouldn't be using this in the hospital. It's breaking the rules.'

'So I've been told. Trouble is, I've never been much good with rules.'

Her beautiful mouth flickered into a tiny smile of mutual understanding. 'That's one thing we have in common, then. But while you're in here, you have to behave.'

'Discharge me and I'll behave. So—has he found me a nurse?'

'Not a nurse, exactly.'

'What's that supposed to mean? I have to have someone who knows what they're talking about. And preferably someone who doesn't call me Your Highness at the end of every sentence.'

He needed to get out of here before lying here trapped with his own thoughts drove him crazy. He needed distraction.

Tasha lifted her head. Her gaze connected with his. '*I* know what I'm talking about. And I have no intention of calling you Your Highness.'

'You?' Alessandro felt shock thud through his gut. 'You're a children's doctor.' She was also someone he'd carefully avoided for over a decade.

'I'm a doctor. My speciality just happens to be children. But I have all the skills necessary to assist your rehabilitation. I can nag you to do your exercises, throw away the junk food and make sure you take lots of healing early nights—' humour lightened her voice '—on your own. I've never been anyone's nurse before but I'm a quick study.'

His mouth felt dry but he was in too much pain to try and reach for his glass again. 'You're offering to nurse me?'

'We're old friends, Alessandro. It's the least I can do.' Her smile was warm and genuine, so why did he feel so uneasy?

Something didn't feel right.

He decided that this was one of those occasions that merited the direct approach. 'You and I, we didn't exactly part on good terms.'

'No. You were a complete bastard,' she said frankly, 'but that was a long time ago. I was at an impressionable age. Do you honestly think I'm still bothered about something that happened almost ten years ago? That would be ridiculous, don't you think?'

Would it?

He looked at her for a long moment, his eyes searching out the true sentiment behind the lightly spoken words. 'Tasha—'

She leaned towards him, mockery in her gaze. 'I was seventeen years old. I had no taste, and I was overwhelmed by the fact that you were a prince. And now we've got that out of the way, can we just forget it? No girl should be made to feel embarrassed about the foolish crushes she had as a teenager. So what do you say, Alessandro? Am I hired?'

Josh opened the front door of his house, his mood swerving between elation and guilt.

He tried to push the guilt back where it belonged.

His marriage to Rebecca was over. She was the one who had called time on their relationship and moved out. They'd wanted different things.

Right through their relationship, they'd wanted different things.

As he hung up his jacket Megan's fragrance engulfed him, wrapping him in memories.

Maybe he'd moved on a bit quickly, but he was human, and when it came to Megan...

Just thinking about her lifted his mood, and he closed the front door, relieved that Tasha had refused his invitation to come home with him. He needed time to think, but already his mind was racing ahead, thinking of the future. He wanted Megan here, with him, all the time. He wanted to laugh with her over a meal, he wanted to sleep with her and wake up with her. They were adults, weren't they? He was past the age of wanting to creep around like a teenager. Snatched moments in the on-call room would never be enough for him. He knew what he wanted now.

He wanted Megan. In his life. For ever.

Energised by a certainty he'd never felt before, Josh checked his phone, hoping to find a message from her, but there was nothing and he was surprised by the strength of the disappointment that thudded through him.

Had she gone back to sleep after he'd received the call that his sister was in the department? He imagined her still lying there, in sheets tangled from the heat of their loving, dreaming about what they'd shared.

Was she planning even as he was planning?

Pondering that question, he threw his keys on the table, feeling lighter than he had in months. Smiling slightly, he retrieved the post from the floor and strolled into the kitchen, lured by the promise of strong coffee.

'Hello, Josh.' Rebecca sat there, her beautiful face pale, her eyes sharp with accusation.

Reality slapped his dreams in the face.

Josh felt the lightness evaporate and a sick dread that he couldn't identify settled around him like a dark cloak. 'What are you doing here?'

'I'm your wife, Josh.' Her tone was brittle. 'This is still my home.'

Guilt churned inside him. It was hard to remember they'd ever been close. Hard to remember that once they'd chosen each other.

'Where were you last night?'

He bit back the urge to tell her to mind her own business. 'At the hospital. It's where I work.'

'But you weren't working, were you? And don't bother lying to me because I phoned the hospital to ask where you were.' She gave a thin smile. 'Consultant's wife's privileges. No one knew where you were, but they did know you weren't on duty.'

Josh felt as though the walls of the house were closing in on him. Moments ago his future had seemed so clear. Now all he saw was murky black. 'Rebecca—'

'Am I supposed to be grateful that you didn't have sex with her in our bed?' Her fury snapped chunks out of the fragile remains of their relationship. 'Who is she, Josh? And don't bother denying there's someone else because I can see it in your eyes.'

It wasn't just in his eyes. It was in his heart. It was all through him and it gave him strength to do the right thing. *To fight.*

Josh straightened his shoulders. 'There is someone. You and I—our relationship is over, Rebecca. We've agreed that, and—'

'I'm pregnant.'

The silence in the room was absolute. It was as if the words had stopped time but he knew it wasn't the case because the hands of the kitchen clock were still moving.

Pregnant. A baby.

Josh felt strangely detached. The words floated through his numb brain but didn't settle. Pregnant. It was as if he was outside himself, looking in. And then reality punched him in the gut. Denial burst to the surface, driven by a desperate need to hold onto the dream. 'No.' The word was dragged from deep inside him. 'You can't be. That isn't possible.'

'Why? Because it isn't convenient for you? Because it isn't what you want?' Her voice rose. 'I've got news for you, Josh. Babies don't always come along at the most convenient moment in your life.'

He knew that. Just hours ago Megan had finally confirmed that the baby she'd lost so traumatically eight years earlier had been his—a cruel epilogue to the night both of them had spent in hell. His decision to save Megan's life all those years before had cost her a child. Their child. The knowledge intensified a guilt and pain that had never left him.

When he and Rebecca had split, his first thought had been, *Thank goodness we didn't have kids.*

And now…

'You know I don't want children.'

Rebecca's laugh was devoid of humour. 'Maybe you should have thought about that before you had sex with me.' There was a coarseness to her declaration that made him feel like scrubbing his skin.

'That was a mistake.' Josh stood still, the ache in his heart more painful than anything physical that she could inflict on him. Now, with some distance, he couldn't imagine why they'd had sex again. What had driven him back into her bed? His brain tried to drag out details from that night but all he remembered was her, urging him on... 'Did you do it on purpose?' Blind with pain, he shot the words at her, wanting the truth even though he knew it wouldn't change the facts. The colour in her cheeks answered his question and he swallowed down the bitter taste of contempt. 'You chose to bring a child into a dead, loveless marriage?'

'You chose to have sex with me,' she said acidly. 'So it's not completely dead, is it? Or maybe you've conveniently forgotten that night.'

No, he hadn't forgotten. The memory sat in his gut, the regret hard and undigested. Of all the mistakes he'd made in his life, that was the biggest. If he could rewind the clock... 'You were taking the Pill.'

'I'm pregnant, Josh. Nothing either of us does or says is going to change that. So before you get too deeply embedded in this exciting new relationship of yours, we need to think what we're going to do. You're going to be a father.'

CHAPTER THREE

As IDEAS went, this had been one of her worst.

Tense and on edge, Tasha paced around Alessandro's stunning, contemporary clifftop home, wishing she'd never agreed to the plan. But refusing would have invited awkward questions from Josh. And anyway, she hadn't thought for a moment that she'd feel anything for Alessandro except mild contempt.

She'd planned to wash the boy out of her hair— she'd forgotten that the boy was now a man. A man who oozed sex appeal and natural authority even when badly injured. From the moment she'd walked into his private room and seen him watching the nurse through those slanting, slightly mocking eyes she'd known she was in trouble.

The nerves jumped in her stomach and she realised how long it had been since she'd been around a man who had that effect on her. The few relationships she had, she was careful to keep light and casual. She preferred it that way.

Her usual confidence deserting her, Tasha kept her back to him and focused her attention on the house. The place was incredible. Built on one level, floor-to-ceiling glass wrapped itself around the house, giving uninterrupted views over the beach from every angle of the living room. Deep soft sofas in ocean colours grouped around a large blue-and-white-striped rug and there were touches of the sea everywhere. Elegant pieces of driftwood. An old anchor. And then there were the paintings and the books.

Tasha glanced in envy at the bookshelves and wished she had a free month to read her way through the collection while lying on one of those squashy sofas and occasionally looking at the view. Somehow the place managed to be stylish and contemporary while maintaining a cosy, intimate feel.

'How on earth did you find this place?'

'I knew where I wanted to live. When this house came up, someone tipped me off.'

Knowing how much property cost in this part of the world, Tasha gave a wry smile. 'I dread to think how much you paid.'

'The real problem was planning permission.

The original house was structurally unsound and we had to persuade them that this would enhance the landscape.'

Tasha glanced up at the double height living room, awash with light. 'Your architect was clever.'

The view alone would have fetched millions. Outside, a wide deck curved around the house, a glass balustrade offering some protection while ensuring that not a single element of the outdoors was lost. The home shrieked style and sophistication. And then there were the gadgets…

It was a contemporary palace, she thought, *fit for a playboy prince.*

The evidence of wealth was everywhere and the high-tech security meant there was no forgetting the identity of her patient. From the moment the electronic gates had opened onto the long winding drive that led up to the clifftop house, she'd been aware of the security cameras. And then there was the team of highly trained security staff who worked shifts protecting the prince.

Tasha risked a glance at him and thought to herself that he didn't look like a man who needed anyone's protection. From the dark stubble on his jaw to the dangerous gleam of his eyes, he was more pirate than prince.

It occurred to her that she'd only ever met him in her world. Never in his. She'd never thought of him like this, with protection officers on twenty-four-hour rotation.

At seventeen she'd been in awe of the fact that he was actually a prince, but she'd never thought about what that really meant. To her, the word 'prince' made her think of fairy-tales. Of chivalry, bravery and honour. To a little girl whose father had walked out, those qualities had seemed like riches. She still remembered her reaction when Josh had told her his university friend was coming to stay. Her mouth had dropped open and she'd said those words that afterwards she'd regretted for years. *'A real, live prince?'* From that moment onwards she'd been doomed to a lifetime of teasing by her older brothers, but at the time she hadn't even cared. Meeting a prince had been the ultimate romantic experience for a teenager just discovering boys. Her brain had taken up permanent residence in dreamland. Right from the day he'd stepped out of his armoured car, the sun gleaming off his glossy dark hair, she'd carried on dreaming. At twenty, Alessandro Cavalieri had been insanely handsome, but what had really drawn her had been his charm. Used to being on the receiving end of nothing but verbal abuse from her brothers and their friends, his charisma had been fascinating and compelling. Instead of treating her as a tomboy, he'd treated her as a woman. She'd never stood a chance.

She'd dreamed her way through countless lessons, concocting scenarios where Alessandro ignored all the beautiful girls who threw themselves at him because he couldn't look at anyone but her. The reality had been so far removed from the fantasy that the inevitable crash between the two had been catastrophic.

Reminding herself of that fact settled the nerves in her stomach. True, he was even more spectacular to look at now, but she was no longer a dreamy, romantic teenager. Neither was she interested in a relationship with a man whose only commitment was to his own ego. She was past the age when a handsome face was the only thing she noticed.

Relieved to have rationalised the situation, Tasha started to relax. 'The view of the beach is good. The surfing here is some of the best in Cornwall and it's never busy because of the rocks. You have to know what you're doing.'

'Josh told me you all used to spend hours surfing here when you were kids.'

'It used to drive our mother out of her mind

with worry.' She rested her head against the glass. 'It's been so long since I surfed.'

'That surprises me. I can't imagine you working in a city.'

'That's where the job was.' *Was.* Tasha felt a ripple of panic but masked it quickly. 'Anyway, it feels good to be home. Familiar.'

'There's a private path from the terrace that leads straight down onto the beach. It's the reason I bought this property. You can surf from the front door. Did you bring your wetsuit?'

'Of course.' Tasha thought about the suitcases in her car. She was like a snail, she thought, carrying her world around on her back. And what was she doing, talking surfing with him? The point of this wasn't to be intimate or cosy. Deciding that it was never too soon to start inflicting a little extra pain, she gave a sympathetic smile. 'Shame you can't join me.'

'Thanks for the reminder.' The irritation in Alessandro's voice confirmed that her arrow had found its target.

'At least I'll be able to get out there and surf, and I'll give you a report,' Tasha said kindly, feeling a flash of satisfaction as she saw his jaw tighten. *Oh, boy, are you going to suffer.* She was about to twist the knife again when he shifted position and she saw pain flicker in his eyes. His naturally olive skin was several shades paler than usual and she could see the strain in his face. The physician in her at war with the woman, Tasha strolled over to him. 'Moving you from the hospital to here must have been a painful experience.'

'It was fine.'

He hadn't uttered a word of complaint but she knew that he must have been in agonising pain. 'I'll try and help you find a comfortable position.'

'I'm perfectly comfortable. And I don't need your help.'

'That's why you're paying me, remember? To help you. You need a nurse to look after you.'

'I needed a nurse because they wouldn't discharge me from hospital without one. Not for any other reason.' Jaw clenched, Alessandro manoeuvred himself onto the sofa, the pain involved leaving him white-faced. The muscles of his shoulders bunched as he took his weight on the crutches. 'I don't need to be looked after.'

Tasha found herself looking at those muscles. Pumped up. Sleek and hard. She frowned. *So what?* It took more than muscles to make a real man. 'So if you don't need to be looked after, what am I expected to do? File my nails?'

'You can do whatever you like. Read a book.

Watch TV. Surf—although if that's how you spend your day, I'd rather you didn't tell me about it.' He dropped the crutches onto the floor with a clatter that said as much about his mood as the black frown on his face. 'Do whatever you like. Consider it an all-expenses-paid holiday.'

But she wouldn't choose to take a holiday with him, would she?

Ten years had done nothing but add to his physical attractions, she thought irritably. It was all very well reminding herself that looks didn't count, but everything about him was unapologetically masculine and being alone with him made her feel jittery. Which was ridiculous, she told herself, given that he could barely walk. He was hardly going to leap on her, was he? Anyway, he'd made it clear years before that he didn't find her attractive.

Reminded of the 'flat-chested' comment by her brother, it was all she could do to stop herself thrusting her chest forward. 'Now that I'm here, you might as well at least let me fetch you a drink.'

'Thanks. A drink would be good.' The tension in his voice reflected the pain he was fighting. 'Whisky is in the cupboard in the kitchen and you'll find glasses on the top shelf. Join me.

We'll have drinks on the terrace if I can get myself there.'

Drinks on the terrace?

Tasha felt a flash of alarm. No way. Lounging on the deck, watching the sun go down over golden sand was far too intimate a scenario. That wasn't what she had in mind at all. This was about inflicting pain, not taking pleasure. Not that she thought she was in any danger of falling for him again, but as a scientist reviewing the evidence she had to concede that it had happened before.

'A drink sounds like a good idea, but forget the terrace. You only just sat down, and if you keep moving you'll just make the pain worse.' Whisky, she thought, laced with arsenic or something equally poisonous. Or maybe just whisky along with the powerful painkiller and antibiotics he'd been prescribed. It would knock him unconscious and then she wouldn't need to worry about falling for his dangerous charm.

Not that he seemed charming right now. Pain had made him irritable and moody and he leaned his head back against the sofa, jaw clenched, eyes closed. 'I'll have it straight. No water. No ice.'

In other words, nothing to dilute the effects of the alcohol.

Tasha walked into the kitchen, knowing that every movement she made was being followed by those fierce black eyes. She remembered him telling her that his ancestors had been warriors, descendents of the Romans who had once colonised the Mediterranean island of San Savarre that was his home. It was all too easy to imagine Alessandro Cavalieri in warrior mode.

Irritated with herself, shrugging off those thoughts, she opened cupboards until she found whisky. Closing her hand around the bottle, she hesitated. It would be really bad for him to drink with the tablets, but Alessandro didn't seem to care. Clearly he was seeking oblivion. He'd drink whisky and to hell with the consequences. In fact, he'd probably enjoy the experience of alcohol and painkillers. Tasha put the bottle back. She wasn't here to do what he wanted. She wasn't here to make his life comfortable. It was already comfortable enough.

She glanced around her. The kitchen was like something from an upmarket show home. Light poured through a glass atrium and reflected off shiny black granite work surfaces. It was smooth and streamlined, designed for practicality as well as show.

'I could almost want to cook in a place like

this,' Tasha muttered, yanking open the door of the tall American fridge and staring at the contents. 'Nothing but champagne and beer—typical man. What about food?' Exploring the lower shelves, she found some mouldy cheese and a dead lettuce, which she removed and dropped in the bin. 'Good job I went to the supermarket.'

While the ambulance crew had been preparing Alessandro for the transfer home, she'd taken herself into St Piran on a shopping trip for provisions. She'd spent several hours carefully selecting items to help her with her plan, thinking carefully about what would help her cause. Abandoning the idea of using anything from his fridge, she reached for her bag of supplies and pulled out a packet of herbal tea.

Perfect.

She'd yet to meet a man who enjoyed herbal tea.

Humming happily, Tasha boiled water and found two mugs.

Carrying the tea back to the living area, she put the tray down on the low glass table and waited expectantly.

The wait was worth it. His reaction was everything she'd hoped for.

Alessandro stared in disbelief at the pale

yellow liquid steaming in the mugs. 'What the hell is that?'

'Herbal tea,' Tasha said earnestly. She groped around for something convincing to say about it. 'It will be good for you. It boosts the immune system and works as a—as a—as an internal cleanser.' As a highly trained clinician, she couldn't believe she was spouting such un-scientific nonsense and she braced herself for Alessandro to burst out laughing and demand she show him the data to support her claims, but he didn't. Instead he glowered at her, his eyes narrowing to two dangerous slits.

'Is this a joke? This is your idea of taking care of me?'

'Absolutely. I'm doing what's good for you.'

'Whisky would be good for me.'

Tasha made an attempt at a timid smile. Given that she'd never done 'timid' before in her life, she was reasonably pleased with the result. 'Don't be angry,' she coaxed. 'I remembered afterwards that the whisky won't go well with painkillers and antibiotics so I went for tea instead. I'm sup-posed to be looking after your health, remem-ber? That's why I'm here. Try it. It's delicious. Caffeine-free and *so* healthy.'

His gaze slid from her eyes to the contents of

the mug. 'It looks like something that's come straight from the drains.'

'Really? I find it delicious.' To prove her point, Tasha took an enormous gulp of hers and just about managed not to spit it out. *Utterly vile.* 'Mmm. Are you sure I can't tempt you?'

'Is that a serious question?' The dangerous gleam in his eyes was a reminder to Tasha not to underestimate him. He wasn't tame. And he wasn't a pussy cat. He was a man who was used to controlling everyone and everything around him.

And it was clear to her now that he really didn't want anyone there. He'd only agreed to it to facilitate his early discharge.

She gave a faint smile. That was good, wasn't it? She didn't want him to want her here. That was the whole point. She was here to make his life difficult and uncomfortable while proving to herself that his charm had just been the creation of her hormonal teenage brain. So far she was doing well.

Apart from that initial jolt she'd felt when she'd first seen him lounging in the hospital bed, she had herself well under control.

She ignored the tiny voice inside herself that warned her she was playing with fire—that however dangerous he'd been as a boy, the threat was magnified now he was a man.

Handing him a glass of water, she kept up the sympathy. 'Take your antibiotics and painkillers now and then you can have another lot before you go to bed.' Unable to switch off the doctor inside her, she frowned at his leg. 'You should keep that elevated. Wait a minute…' She grabbed three cushions from one of the sofas and carefully repositioned his leg. Although she was gentle, she knew the pain had to be agonising, but Alessandro didn't murmur and she felt a flash of grudging respect. At least he wasn't a wimp or a whiner. 'How does that feel?'

'As if a horse trampled on it?' His dry humour bought a smile to her lips but she killed it instantly, unsettled by the ease with which the smile had come. She didn't want to find him amusing any more than she wanted to find him attractive. And then her eyes met his and the desire to smile faded instantly.

Sexual tension punched through her, stealing her breath and clouding her mind. The power of it shook her.

'Take your tablets,' she croaked. She wanted to look away but there was something about those sexy dark eyes that wouldn't allow it.

How long they would have stayed like that she didn't know because the phone suddenly buzzed, breaking the spell.

'Leave it,' he said roughly, but Tasha was relieved and grateful for anything that gave her an excuse to turn her back on him. She felt dizzy. Light-headed—as if she were floating.

'It could be someone important.' Her hand shook slightly as she picked up the phone. *Note to self,* she thought. *Don't look at the guy unless you have to.* 'Hello?'

A woman's voice came down the phone, smooth and sultry.

The dizziness faded in an instant and Tasha thrust the phone at him, plummeting back to earth with a bump. 'It's for you. Someone called Analisa. She doesn't sound too happy.' *And that made two of them.* Clearing the tray, Tasha stomped back into the kitchen.

What the hell was she playing at? Staring at a guy like some sort of dreamy teenager!

Scowling, she tipped the herbal tea down the sink.

If she'd needed reminding what Alessandro was like, it was that phone call.

She didn't understand the language, but it was obvious that Alessandro wasn't spending time placating the woman. Judging from his bored tone, it wasn't going to bother him if Analisa or whatever her name was didn't phone back.

And that, Tasha thought angrily, summed up Alessandro Cavalieri. He didn't care how many women he hurt. Flirt today, dump tomorrow.

She took her time in the kitchen and by the time she strolled back into the living room, Alessandro was no longer on the phone. 'Did you take those tablets?'

'Yes. They would have gone down more easily with whisky.'

'You're going to need a clear head to handle all those women who keep calling you.'

'Are you jealous?'

'Oh, please!' Tasha moved the crutches out of the way before he tripped and did more damage. 'Don't flatter yourself. Fortunately for both of us, I've grown out of the girl-meets-prince fantasy.'

'Good, because girl-meets-prince has never done anything for me. It's all fake.' His tone was irascible and suddenly she wished she'd stayed in the kitchen.

The house was huge, and yet suddenly it seemed small.

It was all too intimate, too—*terrifying?*

'You're very bad-tempered. That's probably because you're hungry. If you're sure I can't tempt you with some of my lovely, delicious tea, I'll go and make us some supper instead.'

'You'd better phone for a take-away because there isn't anything in the fridge.'

'Actually, there was, but most of it looked ready for a post mortem so I threw it away. The only thing within use-by date in your fridge is the champagne, and last time I looked that wasn't listed as one of the five major food groups.' Ignoring the empty space on the sofa next to him, she sprawled in one of the chairs, curling her legs underneath her. 'I gather you don't cook.'

'I have a chef, but while I've been in hospital I gave him time off.'

A chef? 'Yes, well, next time tell him to clean the dead bodies out of the fridge before he leaves. Lucky for you I had the foresight to pick up some food on the way so we're not going to starve.'

'I don't expect you to cook. That isn't why you're here.' His face was paper white and she could see that the slightest movement caused him agony. 'Anyway, I'm not hungry.'

'If you don't eat, you won't recover. Why do you have a chef?'

'I'm a useless cook. And I'm usually too busy to cook. I eat out a lot.'

With women like the sultry Analisa. 'Well, that's not a problem. It will be my pleasure to make you delicious treats.' Generally she hated cooking, but Tasha decided not to share that with him. She'd already decided what she was cooking him for dinner. 'In fact, why don't I get started? You ought to have an early night.'

'I'm not big on early nights.' Those dark eyes found hers. 'Unless there's a reason.'

'A broken ankle and bruised ribs are a reason.' Rejecting the chemistry, Tasha uncurled her legs and stood up. 'The body heals better when it's rested.'

'So you're good in the kitchen?'

'I'm good in every room, Alessandro.' Leaving him to dwell on that comment, Tasha walked back to the kitchen and closed the door firmly behind her.

The irony didn't escape her. Normally she avoided the kitchen. Here, it felt like a refuge from Alessandro.

Trying not to think about him, she emptied her bags over the shiny black work surface and picked up a small bag of extra-hot chillies.

Stir-fry, she thought, *with a kick.*

She couldn't kick him herself, but this should do the job for her.

But as she chopped and sliced she discovered that it was impossible not to think about him. And thinking made her wonder about the dark clouds she saw in his eyes. She'd been a doctor long enough to recognise when someone was suffering. And she didn't think the dark emotions swirling around him had anything to do with the accident.

Might have caused the accident, though, she mused, slicing onion with surgical precision.

Minutes later she had noodles cooking in boiling water and she was stir-frying a generous quantity of garlic, red chilli and ginger. Making a guess at the timing, Tasha gamely tipped in vegetables and juicy prawns and finally added the noodles.

As it sizzled, she turned to the other pan and stirred the contents. It looked identical except for one ingredient—it lacked the copious amounts of red chilli.

Just don't mix them up, she reminded herself as she plated the meal, adding a touch of garnish to make the dish extra appetising.

Pleased with the result, she walked through to the light, airy living room. The sun had dipped below the horizon and the evening was cool. Alessandro lay sprawled on the low sofa where she'd left him, staring with brooding concentration at the waves crashing onto the shore.

'The first time I surfed here I was twenty. Josh brought me.'

And she'd followed them. Egged on by her best friend from school, they'd hidden, giggling, behind the rocks, watching as her brother and his sexy friend stripped down to board shorts.

Tasha put the plates down on the table with a clatter. 'I would have thought a playboy with a private jet and your surfing skills would have chosen North Beach, Hawaii, or Jeffreys Bay in South Africa.'

'I love Cornwall. Staying with your family was one of the happiest times of my life.'

The words pushed her control off centre and Tasha felt her stomach lurch. It had been the happiest time of her life, too. Which had made the abrupt ending even harder. 'Our home wasn't exactly big—it must have felt like a shoebox to you after palace life.'

'It felt like a proper home. And I envied the way you could all just get on with your lives without having to think about crowds and security.'

As a teenager she'd thought it was impossibly glamorous having security guards, but now she could see that it might be an inconvenience, especially for an active, athletic guy like Alessandro.

'I guess Cornwall is a pretty low-profile place.'

'It's not bad. Fortunately this house isn't too accessible. How often do you surf?'

'Me?' Tasha handed him cutlery. 'Not as often as I'd like to because I generally work long hours. Normally, that's the way I like it. I'm a career girl. But now that I'm looking after you...' she shrugged '...I intend to make up for lost time.'

'So if you're a career girl, how come you're not working right now?'

Unwittingly he'd tapped into her deepest fears. That she might not be able to find another job. *That her altercation with her last boss might have blown her reputation to smithereens.*

Tasha opened her mouth and closed it again, unsettled by the sudden desire to confide. She stifled it, knowing that confiding was the first step towards intimacy. And she didn't want intimacy with this man. 'I'm in between jobs. I've cooked a stir-fry. I hope that's all right with you.'

'Looks delicious.' He picked up a fork. 'I can imagine you as a children's doctor.'

'I'll take that as a compliment. Do you want to try and eat at the table?'

'No, this is fine. You're right that moving

around hurts. I think the journey to the bedroom will be enough of a challenge for one evening.'

As he shifted position, her eyes were drawn to his body.

No man had a right to be so good looking, Tasha thought as she registered the strength in those wide shoulders. It should have been enough that he was a prince. And rich. Looking like a sex god as well was just too many gifts for one person.

She might have been irritated if it hadn't been for the fact he was about to eat her food. And that was going to be a real test of manhood.

Hiding a smile, Tasha turned her attention back to her own plate. 'I love your kitchen. The design is fantastic. A whole different experience for me. Dinner for me is usually a cardboard sandwich from the hospital cafeteria at three in the morning.'

'It didn't look anything like this when I bought it. The rooms were small and the whole place was pretty dark. I worked with an excellent architect and we knocked down almost every wall, put in the skylights…' He glanced up at the roof of the double-height sitting room. 'We decided it was worth gutting the place because it had such potential. We opened it up, let the light flow in. This is delicious, by the way. You're a good cook.'

Delicious? *He thought it was delicious?*

Tasha stared at him in disbelief. 'You like it?'

'After two weeks of hospital food?' He twisted noodles around his fork with skill and precision. 'This is heaven.'

He had to be kidding. It had to be a double bluff. Unless…

Tasha stared down at her own plate. Had she mixed them up?

Cautiously, she took a mouthful, waiting for her mouth to explode into flames from the chilli, but the flavours in her food were subtle and she knew instantly she didn't have the wrong plate. Which meant he clearly had a mouth lined with asbestos.

'Is there any more?' Alessandro speared the last prawn. 'You don't seem to be eating yours.'

'I am. And there isn't any more.' She hadn't thought for a moment he'd eat what she'd served him. Clearly his mouth was as tough as the rest of him.

Feeling aggravated, Tasha finished her food. 'Why did you fall anyway? Was the horse too difficult for you?'

He accepted the slight with a flicker of a smile.

'The horse wasn't difficult. I lost concentration for a moment, but that was long enough for the guy on the opposite team to bring us down. My ankle took most of the weight. My ribs took the rest.' He leaned back against the sofa, his eyes closed.

She wondered why he'd lost concentration.

'You were trapped under the horse? Ouch. So no physical activity for the rest of the summer?'

His eyes opened and he studied her from underneath lush, dark lashes. 'Depends what you mean by physical activity.'

Staring into those dangerous dark eyes, her mouth dried. 'I meant polo and surfing.' Tasha felt the heat slowly spread through her body and wished she'd never mentioned physical activity. Even injured, the man was deadly. 'You look tired. Do you want me to call your security team to help you from the sofa to the bed?'

'No. I have the crutches and I can manage.'

'Independent, aren't you?'

'You could say that.'

Torn between wanting to see him suffer and not wanting him to exacerbate his injuries, Tasha tilted her head. 'The crutches won't be much use while your ribs are so bruised. We might need to think of other options.'

'This is fine.' Shifting to the edge of the sofa, Alessandro picked up the crutches and stood up, taking his weight on his good leg.

Tasha flinched.

That had to hurt.

'Alessandro—'

'I can do it. Just give me space.' There was a stubbornness in his tone. A grim determination to succeed despite the agonising pain. Reluctantly impressed, Tasha stood there, careful not to touch him and distinctly unsettled by how much she wanted to do just that.

'Look, I could call one of those burly security guards—'

'It would help if you could check the route to my bedroom is clear. So far I haven't mastered doing this with obstacles.' His face was chalk-white as he slowly eased his way forward. 'I'll just use the bathroom on the way so that I don't have to make two journeys.'

Tasha watched as the muscles in his powerful shoulders flexed and knew that every movement had to be causing him agony. 'I think you need help.'

He cast her a look that told her he'd be long dead before he'd accept help from anyone. A crooked smile flickered at the corners of his mouth. 'You're offering to assist me in the bathroom? Now, that could be interesting.'

Trying to work out how the atmosphere had shifted to intimate, Tasha felt her face turn scarlet. 'I just don't see how you're going to manage to do what you have to do without help.'

His eyes lingered on hers for a long moment. Mockery mingled with something else that she didn't even want to put a name to. 'You want to come and watch how it's done, *tesoro*?'

He'd called her that at seventeen and her heart rushed forward, doubling its rhythm. '*Don't* speak Italian.'

'Why not?'

'Because…' Her mouth was dry. 'Because I don't speak it and it's rude to talk a language someone doesn't understand.'

'It's my native tongue.'

'I know. But you're fluent in English so that's no excuse.' She scowled at him. 'I just don't want you falling and fracturing more bones. I'm not sure my patience with this whole nursing thing is going to last that long, so you'd better heal quickly.'

He shifted the position of the crutch. His knuckles were white where they gripped the handles. 'I won't lock the door. If I find myself in trouble,

I'll shout and you can come to my rescue. But not on a white charger. I've had enough of horses for one week.'

Pinned to the spot by that dark, sexy gaze, Tasha felt as if she were the one who had eaten the chilli. Her entire body was caught in a fiery rush of heat and suddenly she didn't feel like the one in control. 'Fine,' she croaked, 'leave the door unlocked. Good idea.'

Feeling the heat in her face, she moved through to his bedroom and cleared the suitcase off the bed. His bed was enormous and faced out towards the sea.

How many hearts had he broken in that bed?

Trying to push aside disturbing images of Alessandro's strong body tangled with a slender female frame, Tasha ripped the duvet back so that he could get into the bed and wondered why on earth she'd volunteered for this job. Why had she ever thought she could make his life difficult? The herbal tea had been moderately irritating but the chilli hadn't even registered on his taste buds, and all her digs about surfing hadn't had much impact either.

And now she was stuck here with a man who made her think things she didn't want to think. It had always been like that, she remembered crossly, even as a teenager. When Alessandro had walked into the room there had never been any confusion. She'd known she was a woman.

If she really wanted him to suffer then she needed to do something drastic.

What was a man like Alessandro likely to be missing more than anything?

Tasha gave a slow smile as she thought about the other items in her shopping bags.

Time for Plan B.

The pain in his ribs was excruciating. Even small movements resulted in blinding agony, as if a burning-hot poker was being forced into his chest.

But at least it distracted him from the parts of his life he was trying to forget.

Taking advantage of the privacy of the bathroom, Alessandro gave in to the pain.

He balanced himself against the washbasin and reached for a glass. To add to the pain in his ribs and his ankle, his mouth felt as though someone had started a bonfire. Chilli, he thought, gulping down water. When he'd taken the first mouthful of food he'd thought she must have made a mistake but then he'd seen her eating hers happily. Clearly she liked her food hot. Not wanting to offend her, he'd forced his down, eating it as quickly as possible. If she walked out, he'd be back in hospital and there was no way he was going back to hospital. So he'd forced himself to eat with enthusiasm the food she'd prepared.

He drank deeply, wondering how long it took nerve-endings to recover. There wasn't a single part of his body that wasn't burning.

Frustrated by his own weakness, accustomed to being at the peak of physical fitness, Alessandro used the bathroom and then clenched his jaw against the pain and hobbled back towards the bedroom, trying in vain to find some way of distributing his weight so that the movement didn't exacerbate his injuries.

Tasha had turned back the duvet and smoothed the sheets.

Never before had his bed looked so inviting, but the short distance from the door felt like running a marathon. It didn't help that she was watching him, those cool eyes steady on his face.

'Aren't you taking your nursing duties a little too seriously?' He wished she'd turn away so that he could give in to the pain. 'You're off duty once I go to bed.'

'I'd better help you undress.'

Was she serious? Marvelling at the discovery

that extreme pain didn't seem to interfere with sexual arousal, Alessandro gritted his teeth. For his own sanity he knew he didn't dare let her touch him. 'I'll manage.'

'How? At least let me help you change your shirt for pyjamas.'

'I don't own pyjamas.'

'I thought you might say that, so I bought you some when I was out shopping.' Pleased with herself, she picked up a bag and produced a pair of pyjamas.

Distracted from the ache in his loins by the flash of vivid colour, Alessandro blinked. *'Pink?'*

'It was the only colour they had.' Her expression was anxious. 'Oh, dear. Are you one of those guys who believes wearing pink makes them less masculine? Sorry. I hadn't thought of that. Only I know some guys wear pink shirts these days and I thought these might be OK…'

Was she winding him up? His swift glance at her face suggested nothing but concern. Wondering just how far he was going to have to go not to offend her, Alessandro reminded himself that without her he'd be back in hospital.

Her generosity was the reason he'd be sleeping in his own bed tonight.

All he had to do was keep his hands off her.

Which shouldn't be that hard, surely, given that every movement was agony.

'I don't have a problem with pink.' He eyed the pyjamas in disbelief, wondering which idiot had thought there was a market for such a vile creation. 'But I don't think they'll fit over the cast.'

'Leave that to me.' Beaming at him, she picked up a pair of scissors and cut a slit down one of the legs. 'There. Simple.'

Reflecting on the fact that the wretched garment now looked more like a dress than trousers, Alessandro manoeuvred himself onto the bed and let the crutches fall to the floor. Pain lanced his side and he sat still, breathing slowly, hoping it would pass. The helplessness was driving him mad.

'I'll help you take off your shirt.' Tasha sat next to him on the bed and gently eased off his shirt. As she exposed his chest, the breath hissed through her teeth. 'I've never seen bruises like those, Alessandro. How are you still walking around?' Her tone altered dramatically. Light and flirty gave way to crisp concern.

'I'm fine. To be honest, walking isn't any more painful than breathing.' He was taken aback by the change in her. The girl had gone and in her place was a doctor. A concerned doctor. Her fingers gently traced the bruises and when he glanced at her face he saw that her expression was serious.

'Does this hurt?'

'No.'

She gave him an impatient look. 'Honest answers only, please. A man wearing pink is allowed to express his true emotions even if the resulting language is colourful.'

'All right. It hurts like crazy and I want to punch something?'

'And when I do this?' She pressed lower down and Alessandro swore long and fluently.

'OK.' She didn't blink. 'Now I know you're telling the truth.'

The pain was a blinding, agonising flash. Once again he had that sick dread that the doctors might have missed something. Something that was going to keep him bedridden for longer than a fractured ankle and a few broken ribs. 'Are you trying to kill me?' He spoke through his teeth and she straightened, her hair sliding over her shoulders.

'Actually, no. I'm checking you over. I don't like the look of those bruises. Just sit still. I'm going to check your breath sounds.'

'I've already been examined by about a hundred doctors. They kept wheeling in yet another expert to give an opinion.'

'Sorry, but the only opinion I trust is my own.' She disappeared and reappeared a moment later with a stethoscope in her hand. 'Good job I packed this in my box of tricks, although I haven't listened to an adult's chest for quite a while.'

'If that's supposed to fill me with confidence, it doesn't.' It was a lie. Strangely enough, he was relieved to have her opinion. He remembered Josh telling him that Tasha had astonishing instincts to go with her sharp brain. He had no doubt that she was a skilled doctor. Unfortunately that didn't make things any easier and he sat still while she touched the bruising, trying not to think about how her fingers felt on his skin. 'Do you have to prod me?'

'I'm checking there's no underlying trauma. Those bruises are very impressive. Must hurt a lot.'

Alessandro spoke through his teeth. 'Not at all.' As if the pain wasn't enough, he also had the extra hit of sexual arousal. As she tilted her head, her hair slid forward and brushed against his arm. He tried to move backwards but every movement felt as though he were being slammed into a wall.

'Bones have a lot of nerve-endings,' she murmured. 'That's why it's painful.'

'Thanks for the explanation.'

'Generally, when someone breaks a bone, the treatment is to immobilise it. We can put your ankle in a cast to protect it. Unfortunately we can't do the same thing for your ribs.' Tasha put the stethoscope in her ears. 'Every time you breathe, you hurt yourself again.'

'Can't they strap my chest or something?'

'No. Now stop talking while I listen.' She narrowed her eyes and moved the stethoscope on his chest. Her hair whispered across his arm. 'Breathe in for me.'

Alessandro did and almost passed out. Pain skewered him and darkness flickered around the edges of his vision, muting the lust.

Her eyes locked on his. 'Breathe in and out through your mouth.'

Was she trying to torture him?

But when she finally removed the stethoscope from her ears, her expression was serious. 'Your breath sounds are fine, but I'm going to keep an eye on you. To answer your question, they actually did used to strap chests in the old days, but not any more. It impedes movement and stops you breathing deeply—you can't shift the secretions in your lungs and you can end up with a vile infection. Then you're back in hospital on yet more antibiotics.'

The word 'hospital' was enough to make him ride the pain and breathe deeply. 'I get the message.'

'Don't worry—a young, fit guy like you can cope with a couple of broken ribs and heal quickly. It's older patients who suffer.' Digging her hand into her pocket, she pulled out her phone. 'I'm just going to call your doctor. I want to add in a drug.'

'I'm already swallowing the contents of a pharmacy.'

'I want to give you a non-steroidal alongside your painkillers. I don't know why he didn't give you that. You don't suffer from stomach problems, do you?'

'I've never suffered from anything,' Alessandro growled, 'until a horse fell on me.' Watching Tasha talk on the phone, he found his eyes lingering on the curve of her cheek and the thickness of her eyelashes. She was brisk and professional, giving her opinion bluntly and firmly to a man at least twice her age. Impressive, he thought. And he could imagine her working with children. As a teenager, she'd had an irrepressible sense of fun. Remembering some of the tricks she'd played on her brothers, he allowed himself a faint smile.

'OK, so that's done.' She slid the phone back into her pocket. 'In the morning I'm going to pick you up some extra tablets. I think it will help and so do the guys at the hospital. They should have thought of it, but sometimes it takes a woman to get these things right. Now, then—pyjamas.'

'I can dress without your help.' Alessandro, who had never felt awkward with a woman in his life before, suddenly felt awkward. She was behaving as if they had no history. As if—

Tasha picked up the pink pyjamas and dangled them in front of him, her expression bored.

'I've seen it all before, Alessandro. I'm a doctor.'

'You haven't seen m—' He was about to say that she hadn't seen his body before, but then he remembered that she had. And he'd seen hers. *All of hers.*

And he didn't want to mention that. If she was going to act as if nothing had happened, so was he.

He looked at her cautiously, but her face revealed nothing but professional concern.

'I want to examine the rest of you. Lie back for me.' Her expression serious, her hands moved down his body, sliding and pressing. 'Does this hurt?'

'Everything hurts.' Feeling her cool fingers on his abdomen, Alessandro sucked in a breath. How low did she intend to go?

Lust slammed through him and Alessandro grabbed the duvet and pulled it higher, ignoring the avalanche of pain that rained down on him. 'I'm fine. I can manage. Go to bed. You must be tired.' He wished she'd step back a bit. Her scent was playing havoc with his libido and this close he could see the smoothness of her skin. *How the hell could a guy be aroused when his broken ribs were virtually impaling his lungs*? 'Goodnight, Tasha. Thanks for all your help.'

'If the pain changes, let me know.'

The pain had changed. Suddenly it was all concentrated below his waist and it had nothing to do with being trampled by a four-legged animal. 'Get some sleep.'

'Don't hesitate to wake me up if you need to.' She walked briskly across the room to close the blinds.

'Leave them—I prefer to keep the doors open.'

'You won't be able to sleep.'

He didn't tell her that he rarely slept. 'I'll be fine. I like the fresh air.'

'Well, if you change your mind, just shout out.' Her hips swayed as she walked from window to door. She held a stethoscope in her hand but she walked like a seductress. 'I hope you have a really good night's sleep. I've chosen the bedroom right across the hall and I'll leave the door open so I'll hear you if you shout.'

Great. There were three guest bedrooms, the other two at the far end of the house. Couldn't she have chosen one of those?

After she left, Alessandro spent a frustrating and agonising fifteen minutes removing his shorts. Exhausted, he didn't bother replacing them with the pyjamas. Instead he flopped back against the pillows, drained of energy.

He lay without moving until a noise from across the corridor made him look up.

Tasha was walking across the guest room towards the *en suite* bathroom, undressing as she walked. First she pulled off the scarlet jumper and dropped it in a heap. Her full breasts pushed against a silken wisp of a bra. When her hands moved to the snap of her jeans, Alessandro wanted to groan out a request that she stop, but he couldn't make a sound and the jeans went the way of the jumper and this time the lace was so brief it was almost irrelevant.

His muscles tensed, sending spasms of pain shooting down his bruised body.

Finding it impossible to breathe, Alessandro wondered if one of his broken ribs had suddenly punctured his lung. There was no air in the room. He was suffocating. He lifted his hand to undo his collar and then remembered that he was naked.

As he watched, she stretched upwards to clip her hair on top of her head, the movement accentuating her lean, flat stomach and her long, slim legs. He felt like a voyeur at an erotic floor show. Clearly she'd forgotten that she had both doors open. Either that or she was just assuming he was asleep.

If he called out, he'd embarrass her, and he couldn't look away because his head refused to move.

Telling himself that any moment now she was going to lock the bathroom door, Alessandro kept watching. And he was still watching when she turned her back to him, unfastened her bra and stepped out of her knickers.

CHAPTER FOUR

MEGAN'S hand shook as she opened the door that led to the neonatal intensive care unit.

All day she'd been in a daze of happiness. A daze of happiness that nothing could blunt—not even the knowledge that technically she'd slept with a married man.

Married, but not together, she told herself, wondering why the fact that Josh and Rebecca were almost divorced didn't make her feel any better.

Her head was in a spin and she'd found it almost impossible to concentrate.

She'd thought of nothing else all day, ever since that knock on the door that had sent Josh springing from the bed before they'd had the opportunity to talk about what they'd shared. She had no idea who had been at the door, but whoever it was had been important enough to make sure that Josh didn't return.

Megan had waited for twenty minutes then dressed quickly and exited the on-call room quietly. Her heart had been working double time all the way back to the paediatric ward but she was fairly confident that no one had seen her.

She'd spent the rest of her day stopping herself from checking her phone every two minutes to see if Josh had called. It was like being a teenager all over again.

The extended silence made her jittery and sent her imagination into overdrive.

Was he embarrassed? Did he regret what they'd done?

Reminding herself that Josh was a senior doctor whose working day was ridiculously intense and demanding, she tried to rationalise the fact that he hadn't called. She told herself that it wasn't surprising that he didn't want to publicise their relationship. They were colleagues after all, and affairs between colleagues could so easily become messy.

Having convinced herself that she wasn't likely to see him that day, it came as a shock to see Josh sitting at the computer at the nurses' station.

Megan felt a tiny thrill of excitement bloom inside her.

He wasn't avoiding her. He was here, on her ward.

Her heart pounded against her chest and she

was relieved that the other staff appeared to be occupied elsewhere.

Just for this first encounter she wanted to be alone with him. She didn't want to share the memories of the night with anyone but Josh.

Remembering the look he'd given her just before he'd left the on-call room, she gave a little smile and her stomach fluttered with anticipation.

'Hello, Josh.'

'Ah, Megan, I'm glad you're here. We had an emergency delivery in the department. Thirty-four-weeker.' He turned to her, his tone crisp and professional. 'Showing signs of respiratory distress, so we've transferred him to you.'

There was nothing intimate in his gaze—nothing to hint that they'd spent the night together.

Taken aback, Megan glanced behind her but there was no one within earshot.

The baby was ill, she reasoned, and he was an exceptional doctor. Josh would never put his personal life before the well-being of a patient.

Slowly, she put her bag on the floor, controlling her disappointment. 'Was it a normal delivery?'

As he told her, she found herself looking at his hands and the dark hairs dusting his forearms. Those same hands had touched her. Everywhere. *Held her.* It had been genuine, she had no doubt about that. She still remembered the look in his eyes as he'd driven her wild.

That knowledge gave her confidence. 'Josh—'

'I need to get back.' He rose quickly to his feet, interrupting her before she could finish her sentence. 'You might want to spend some time with the mother. She's very upset. The whole thing took about twenty minutes from start to finish. Precipitate doesn't begin to describe it.'

It was a verbal dismissal but it may as well have been a physical slap for the pain it caused.

'Of course.' Megan pushed the words through stiff lips and stood frozen to the spot as he walked past her, careful not to touch. He was as cold as he'd been eight years before. It was as if their night together hadn't happened.

She wanted to say something. She wanted to grab his arm and demand to know what was going on in his head. She wanted to know why he was hurting her like this.

But his face was a frozen mask and her pride kept her hands by her sides as she let him walk away.

Tasha took her time strolling towards the shower.

He was watching her. She could almost feel the heat of his eyes on her back.

Get a load of that, she thought happily as she stepped into the shower. Flat-chested? *I don't think so.*

From the moment she'd decided to do her strip-tease, her heart had been hammering. First she'd checked he was awake through the crack in the door, then she'd choreographed her walk across the room to ensure that he witnessed every move.

After that all she'd had to do was not give in to temptation and look round. She'd done everything in her power to push up his blood pressure. What she hadn't done was ask herself why she would want to.

Until now.

Muttering to herself, she turned the shower to cold.

Ten years hadn't done anything to make him less attractive. Unfortunately. In fact, he'd filled out in places where it counted. His shoulders were wider, his chest stronger and his arms thickened with muscle. Less of the boy and more of the man. Too much more of the man.

Despite the cold water, her body felt scorching hot again and she wondered why on earth she'd agreed to this.

Another one of her stupid ideas.

She'd thought her feelings for him had been

no more than a childish crush. She'd thought the pain he'd caused would have inoculated her against his lethal charm. She'd thought she was immune. If you'd been infected with something once, you shouldn't catch it again, should you?

So why the explosion of chemistry?

Tasha gave a groan of frustration and turned off the shower.

Her brother was right. She needed to get out more.

Wrapping herself in a huge towel, she opened the bathroom door and risked a glance towards his bedroom. It was in darkness. The feeling of superiority drained out of her. If he'd been watching her, he wasn't now. He wasn't lying there tortured with unfulfilled desire after seeing her in her underwear.

He was asleep.

Which said it all. You couldn't torment a man who didn't even bother looking.

Feeling cross and hot and all sorts of things she didn't want to feel, Tasha flopped onto the bed and rolled onto her stomach, burying her face in the pillow. It wasn't supposed to be this way. She was supposed to have taken one look at him and wondered what she'd seen in him. She wasn't supposed to be having the thoughts she was having now. Why couldn't he be a total wimp like all the other men she met on a daily basis? Her last relationship had floundered after less than a week when the doctor in question had taken to his bed with a dose of man-flu. Tasha, who had endless patience with sick children, had been exasperated by his dying-duck impression but she'd dutifully made hot drinks, dished out tablets and made sympathetic noises until finally calling a halt, reasoning that there was no future in a relationship where one of the partners wanted to strangle the other.

Why couldn't Alessandro provoke the same feelings of irritation?

Why didn't she want to strangle him?

'Ugh.' Blocking out images of his broad shoulders, she burrowed under the pillow. The man had to be in agony. The bruises on his chest were the worst she'd ever seen. But had he uttered a murmur of complaint? No. In fact, he'd been so stoical about the whole thing it had been a struggle to persuade him to take painkillers. She wanted him to be a wimp, but he was anything but. And as for the chilli…

Clearly he liked his food hot.

Tasha thumped the pillow angrily and rolled onto her back. So he was tough. So what? That just proved the man had no nerve-endings and she already knew that. A man with the slightest sensitivity wouldn't have treated her the way Alessandro had treated her.

Had she seen a flicker of remorse?

Had he apologised?

No. And she hadn't exactly progressed in her plan to make him suffer. In fact, so far her plan had totally failed to get off the ground.

Wishing she hadn't wasted her limited finances on sexy underwear, Tasha rolled onto her back and stared at the ceiling.

So far she'd failed spectacularly to make him feel remotely guilty for the way he'd treated her, but she couldn't very well back out now without exposing herself to relentless questioning and teasing by her insensitive brother. Which meant she was stuck here.

She lay in the dark, unable to sleep, wondering how someone with a chest that bruised had somehow managed to get himself to and from the bathroom without help. It hadn't just been the physical strength that had impressed her, it was the mental strength. Somehow he'd pushed through the pain.

He didn't just look like a warrior, he had warrior mentality.

There was a hardness to him that hadn't been there ten years before. He wasn't the same person.

And neither was she.

Tasha was pondering on that when a loud crash echoed around the house.

She was out of bed in a flash, her mind already working through various scenarios. If he'd fallen out of bed, it could have seriously aggravated his injuries. They'd need an ambulance. Paramedics… 'Alessandro?' Sprinting into his bedroom, she saw a lamp lying on the floor where he'd knocked it off the bedside table. On the wall in front of him a football match was being played out on the wide-screen TV and he was watching avidly, his hand locked around the remote control.

'Tash, you're standing in front of the screen!'

'You're watching sport?' Her heart was hammering and she felt weak at the knees. 'You frighten the life out of me and then all you can say is "You're standing in front of the screen"?' Incredulous, she rescued the lamp and waited for her heartbeat to reach a normal level. 'I thought you'd fallen out of bed. I thought you'd broken the rest of your ribs and your skull to go with it.'

'I knocked the lamp off when I was reaching for the remote control.'

SARAH MORGAN 109

'It's two in the morning. What is it with men and the remote control?'

'I wanted to watch sport. I couldn't sleep.'

Him too?

Only she'd been lying there thinking about him while he'd been thinking about football. The knowledge scraped at her nerves and strengthened her resolve. 'Is it the pain?' Tasha straightened the lamp. 'I thought you'd fallen.' And she'd been terrified of what a fall could do to his broken ribs. Not that she cared, she told herself quickly, but she didn't want to be stuck here nursing him any longer than she had to be.

'It isn't pain. Go back to bed, Tasha. I'm sorry I disturbed you.' He didn't shift his gaze from the screen, watching unblinking as the crowd roared its approval. He was a typical man, obsessed with sport, just like her three brothers. She could walk across the room naked and he wouldn't look up because some feat of sporting prowess was being enacted on the giant plasma screen.

Why had she bothered buying expensive lingerie to drive him wild? she thought crossly. She may as well have worn her ancient Mickey Mouse T-shirt.

The glass doors were still open onto the terrace and a cool breeze wafted into the room. 'Shall I close these now?' She walked across the room. 'You must be freezing.'

'I like the cold air.' Something in his tone made her look at him closely and it was only because she was trained to notice subtle clues that she realised he wasn't actually watching the game. True, his eyes were fixed on the screen, but they were blank. Empty.

And suddenly she knew that the football was an excuse.

Tasha switched on the other lamp and for a fleeting second saw the expression on his face. The humour was gone and in its place was exhaustion and pain. She hesitated and then sat down on the chair, hating herself for not just being able to walk away. It wasn't that she cared, she told herself quickly. It was because he was in pain. She'd never been any good at watching someone in pain. 'You look rough.'

'Go to bed, Tasha.' It was a dismissal she chose to ignore.

She wondered whether he was thinking about his injury or the loss of his brother.

'Things always seem worse at night,' she said casually. 'I see it on the ward with both the kids and the parents. There's something about being in the dark. It makes you think too much.' And she knew that sometimes it helped to talk to pass the time. She'd spent hours keeping frightened kids company at night, playing cards, chatting quietly while the rest of the ward slept. 'What were you doing back in Cornwall anyway? I imagined you in some gilded palace, doing prince-like things.'

'You imagined me?' His head turned and she wanted to bite her tongue. Suddenly she was staring into those dark eyes and everything inside her melted, just as it had when she was a teenager.

'Just a figure of speech. You're the crown prince.' Suddenly she felt awkward, and she wondered why she found it so much easier to talk to children than adults. 'I was sorry to hear about your brother. That must have been very hard for all of you.'

'It's life.' His voice was hard and she floundered, wondering how it was possible to want to comfort and run at the same time. 'What are you doing here, Tasha? Why did you really volunteer to look after me?'

Her heart jumped in her chest. So he wasn't just brave, he was as sharp as a blade.

It wouldn't do to forget that.

'I wanted to help.'

'Really?' The bleak, cold look in his eyes had been replaced by smouldering sexuality that made it impossible to breathe or think. Time was suspended. In the background the crowd roared its approval at some amazing feat of sportsmanship but neither of them looked towards the screen. They were looking at each other, the chemistry a magnetic force between them, drawing them together.

And then he turned his head and closed his eyes. 'Go to bed, Tasha.'

Embarrassment drove her to her feet. Another minute and she would have kissed that mouth. She would have leaned forward and—

Oh, God.

'Right. Yes. Good. Well—try not to knock over any more lamps.' She fled to the door, wondering what it was about this man that affected her so badly.

She was a career-woman. She was dedicating her life to her little patients. The only thing she was interested in was getting another job as fast as possible.

This time when she walked into her bedroom she closed the door firmly behind her.

The dark rage inside him mingled with frustration. The inactivity was driving him crazy. Almost as crazy as living with Tasha. Even when she wasn't there, she was there. He smelt her perfume, spied a pair of feminine shoes discarded next to a chair.

And now she was surfing. Alessandro watched from the terrace as she carved into the wave, graceful and perfectly balanced. It was like watching a dancer. Some bolder tourists had chosen to visit the beach to take lessons on the soft sand and then try the bigger surf created by the rocks. They huddled in groups, learning to stand on the board, learning to balance, practising the 'pop-up'. Then they ventured into the water and spent the time falling off their boards in the shallows.

Tasha had none of those problems.

Watching her was sheer poetry. He turned away from the window, envying her the opportunity to push herself physically. Before the accident he would have been out there with her. Or maybe not *with* her, exactly. He frowned, not sure how he felt about having her there. She was the reason he was home, and those new painkillers had certainly taken the edge off the agony. But other parts of him weren't faring so well. The inactivity was driving him mad.

As were the phone calls from Miranda.

She wanted to visit.

But he wasn't ready to see her.

Wasn't ready to make the decision everyone wanted him to make.

Driven by a burning desire to recover as fast as possible, he hauled himself to the bed and started the exercises the physio had shown him.

He worked without rest, channelling all his anger and frustration into each movement, pushing himself hard.

By the time Tasha arrived back in the apartment, he was in agony. Still in her wetsuit, her feet bare, she stood and looked at him.

'Did you take your painkillers before you started?'

It cost him to speak. 'No.'

'That's what I thought. Let me tell you something about pain—once it comes back, it's harder to manage. The trick is to head it off before it returns. You should have waited for me. I was going to do the physio with you.' Dropping her towel and her bag on the floor, she walked over to him. Her hair lay in a damp rope over her shoulder and she smelt of the sea. 'The surf is fantastic.'

Her enthusiasm and sheer vitality sprinkled salt into his wounds. 'I saw you. You took a risk with that last wave.'

'I don't think you're in a position to lecture me about risk given that you lay down under a horse.' She glanced down at his ankle. 'How's that feeling?'

'It's fine, thanks.' Speaking required energy he didn't possess and she gave him a knowing smile.

'Fine? Yeah, I bet. Why don't you sit down and I'll check you over.'

Despite the agony, his entire body heated and he reflected on the fact that having Tasha as his private nurse was the worst torture anyone could have invented. 'You already checked me over.' *And he'd had a sleepless night as a result.*

'Sorry, but while I'm in charge, I'll check you whenever I feel it's necessary.' Cool and calm, she faced him down. 'You're my responsibility. No one dies on my shift, got that?'

'I have no intention of dying.'

'You might, if you carry on being uncoopera-tive.' Her smile managed to be both threatening and sweet as she gestured to the bed. 'Lie down.'

It was an awkward manoeuvre. 'When will they take this damn thing off?'

'That cast is holding your joints in the right position while they heal. When the surgeon is happy that your bones are healing, they'll remove it. Usually about six to eight weeks. So that gives you at least another month. Better get used to it.'

'And once it's removed?'

'Intensive physio—hydrotherapy—'

'Hydrotherapy?'

'Basically exercising in the water.' Gently, she pushed him back against the stack of pillows. 'Good for strengthening muscle without stressing bone and joint.'

Alessandro lay on the bed and tried to ignore the pain licking through his body. He wondered if she planned to change out of the black stretchy wetsuit before she examined him. She looked like Catwoman. 'I just want to be fit.'

'You will be, but it's going to take time.' Tasha reached behind her and unzipped the back of her wetsuit slightly. 'If you're worried that you'll never be fit again, don't be. I've seen your X-rays and I've talked to your surgeon. There's no reason why you won't be back to normal in a few months providing you're sensible. If you do the wrong thing now—if you push it when you should be resting—you'll just do damage. You need to take it steadily and do as you're told.'

Relief mingled with humiliation that she'd read him so easily. 'I'm not good at doing as I'm told.'

If he were, then he'd have bowed to pressure and married.

'I know, but if you want to be fully fit again, that's what you're going to have to do.' Tasha dropped her hands from the zip. 'I need to get out of this gear and take a shower. Then I'll give you a massage to try and relax those muscles of yours. Don't move until I come back.'

'Shower.' Alessandro closed his eyes, not daring to think about the word 'massage'. 'Now you're torturing me.'

She paused, her hand on the doorhandle, a frown in her eyes. 'You could take a shower if you wanted to.'

He gave a sardonic smile and gestured to his cast. 'Oh, yeah—easy as anything.'

'Not easy, but possible. We just have to cover it in plastic to protect it.'

There was a long, pulsing silence. 'You're offering to help me in the shower?'

'That's why I'm here.'

Alessandro wondered if he was the only one feeling warm. Suddenly he wished he hadn't suggested it. Nurse, he told himself. She was offering as a nurse, not anything else. 'I was joking. I can manage.'

'Well, you can't shower on your own, no matter

how macho you are.' Her voice was mild. 'But if you don't want a shower, that's fine. I don't want to push you if you're shy.'

Shy?

It had nothing to do with being shy and everything to do with the fact that she was standing in front of him wearing a form-fitting black wetsuit.

'Yeah.' His voice was a hoarse croak. 'That's right. I'm shy. So we'll give the shower a miss for now.'

As she strolled away from him he took comfort in the fact that at least there was one part of his body that appeared to be working normally.

By the end of two weeks, Tasha had reached screaming pitch.

As plans went, this one had backfired big time.

The tension that had been there on the first day seemed to grow with each passing minute.

If revenge was supposed to be pleasurable then she was definitely doing something wrong because she was in agony. The only one suffering was her.

Instead of giving her the opportunity to be aloof and distant, she was being sucked deeper and deeper into his life. His lack of mobility inevitably meant that she did everything from physio to answering the phone.

Even as she had that thought, the phone rang again and Tasha rolled her eyes and answered it, wondering which of Alessandro's many female friends it would be this time.

A brisk voice informed her that the Princess Eleanor wished to speak to her son, but before Tasha could hand over the phone a cool, cultured voice came down the line.

'Are you his nurse?'

Tasha frowned. 'Well, no, actually, I'm a—'

'Never mind. I'm better off not knowing.' In a cold, unemotional tone she demanded to speak to her son and Tasha passed the phone over without question, feeling defensive and irritated and about as small as a bacterium.

Just what was his mother implying?

She'd been expecting to be asked for a clinical update on progress, but clearly his mother didn't consider her worth speaking to.

Angry with herself for caring, Tasha busied herself tidying up and tried not to listen to the conversation, but it was impossible not to pick up the tension between the two of them, even though the conversation was conducted in Italian.

Alessandro replied to what appeared to be a

barrage of questions in a similar clipped, perfunctory tone and afterwards he flung the phone down onto the sofa, picked up the crutches and struggled onto the terrace. The loud thump of the sticks told her everything she needed to know about his mood.

Startled by the lack of affection between mother and son, Tasha stared at his rigid shoulders for a while and then followed him outside. Was she supposed to say something or pretend it hadn't happened? This wasn't her business, was it? And she wasn't supposed to care…

Torn, she stood awkwardly. 'Can I get you anything?'

'No. Thanks.' He kept his gaze fixed on the surfers in the bay. 'Not unless you can conjure up a new, fit body. I need to heal instantly so that I can get back to my life.'

A life he clearly hated.

'I know it feels frustrating, but if you rush things you'll just do more damage.' She tried to put herself in his mother's shoes. Alessandro was her only surviving son. To hear about his accident must have given her a shock. Perhaps it was anxiety that had put that chill in her tone. 'Your mother must be worried.'

'She's worried I'm not doing my duty. Apparently while I'm "lounging" here, enjoying myself with pretty nurses in attendance—that's you, by the way...' he threw her a mocking smile '...my image is suffering.'

So that explained Princess Eleanor's frigid tone on the phone. She'd assumed there was something going on between the 'nurse' and her son. Irritated rather than embarrassed, Tasha glanced at the bruises visible through the open neck of his polo shirt. 'Does she know how badly you were hurt?'

'Yes. Josh called her while I was in Theatre the first time.'

'And?'

'And she said it was no more than I deserved for indulging in high-risk sports. My accident is badly timed. I had fifty official engagements scheduled over the next month, including opening the annual May ball at the palace.'

'Oh. Well, perhaps she's worried that—'

'Tasha, she isn't worried.' He cut through her platitudes, his dark eyes hard and cold. 'My mother only worries about two things—duty and responsibility. My love of polo was bad enough. Having injured myself, I've committed the cardinal sin of making life very inconvenient for her.'

'You're her son and I'm sure that—'

'Let's get one thing straight.' Alessandro shifted his position so that he was facing her. 'As far as my mother is concerned, the wrong son died. It's because of me that Antonio is no longer Crown Prince. I can't bring him back so I'm expected to fill his shoes…' He hesitated and then muttered something under his breath. 'In every way.'

Tasha frowned. *In every way.* What did he mean by that? 'It wasn't your fault. Why are you blaming yourself?'

He turned away abruptly and Tasha felt the tension flowing from him. Darkness surrounded him like a force field and suddenly she knew that the change in him, the hardness, was all to do with the death of his brother.

Her insides softened. 'Do you want to talk about it?'

'No.'

'But—'

'Not everything can be healed by good nursing, Natasha.' The bitterness sliced through her own defences and she stretched out her hand and touched his arm.

'Is that why she rang? To tell you you've made her life difficult?' Anger glowed inside her and suddenly Tasha wished she hadn't passed him the phone.

She should have screened the call.

'She rang to order me to see my advisers, who apparently have a plan for, and I quote, "pulling something positive" out of this disastrous mess I've made.' A cynical smile tilted his mouth. 'Apparently an injured prince may appeal to a certain age group, so she thinks there may be some mileage in media interviews. So that's my contribution to society—providing entertainment for bored housewives.'

'Next time I'm going to tell her you're asleep and can't be disturbed.' Part of her wondered why she felt the urge to rush to his defence and clearly he was asking himself the same question because he stared at her for a long moment. The hardness left his eyes and he lifted a hand and touched her face. The attraction flickered between them, live and dangerous.

Tasha tried to speak, tried to move, but her body seemed to have shut down and Alessandro gave a low groan, slid his hand behind her head and brought her mouth down on his in a hungry, explosive kiss.

Heat burst through her. Last time she'd kissed him it had been a childish experiment, a desperate desire to grow up fast. There was nothing experimental about this kiss. It was hot and sexual and the explosion of desire gripped her so fiercely that she moaned against his seeking mouth and dug her fingers in the front of his shirt.

It was only as she felt him flinch that she realised how much she must be hurting him. The backs of her fingers were pressed against his bruised chest and she'd leaned into him, instinctively drawing herself closer to his hard body. *Closer to heartbreak.*

'Damn you—no.' Angry with herself, and even more angry with him, she pulled back quickly. 'I didn't want you to do that. I came out here to give you sympathy and support.'

'I don't want sympathy or support. I want you.' He spoke with the assurance and conviction of someone who'd never been turned down by a woman in his life, and she started to shake.

'Don't start that, Alessandro.' She virtually spat the words. 'Don't start all that smooth talk, seduction thing—I'm not interested.'

'Tasha—'

'Age may have given you wider shoulders and longer legs but it obviously hasn't given you a conscience. Do you honestly think I'd put myself through that a second time? Do you think I'm that much of a masochist?' Her voice rose and she saw his dark brows rise in astonishment. 'I'm not interested, Alessandro. I don't want you to kiss me, I don't want you to touch me—' She broke off, aware that her voice was shaking as much as the rest of her. And he was looking at her as if she'd gone mad. *Oh, God, she was overreacting.* She should have laughed it off. Or said she didn't feel anything. Or… Her hands raised, she backed away. 'Coming here was *such* a mistake. I should have said no when Josh asked me. I should have…' She breathed deeply, struggling for control. 'I should have said no.'

'Tasha, wait a minute.' He reached for her but she slapped his hand away and he was forced to grab the rail to regain his balance.

It was a measure of her dedication as a doctor that she made sure he was stable before she walked away.

'Touch me again and I'll break your other leg.' She turned and stalked out off the terrace, her heart crashing against her ribs and terror in her heart.

CHAPTER FIVE

TASHA sat on the bed, her knees drawn up against her chest like a child protecting herself. Her heart was pounding with reaction to the adrenaline surging around her body. The doctor in her recognised the physiological process.

Fight or flight.

The kiss licked like fire through her body, as if that one single touch had set in motion something that couldn't be stopped. She rubbed her hands down her legs, trying to kill the sensations that engulfed her. Why had she let him do that? *Why?*

It wasn't as if she was short on self-discipline. She could say no to chocolate, she'd never been drunk in her life and she'd worked relentlessly to achieve the highest grades possible in her exams. So why couldn't she apply that same single-minded focus to staying detached from Alessandro?

Furious with herself, Tasha thumped her fist on the mattress.

There was something about him that just drew her in. She felt out of her control and that part of it infuriated her more than anything.

Impulse was her greatest fault, she thought savagely. She was a scientist, wasn't she? Impulse shouldn't be part of her make-up, and yet she couldn't seem to stop herself acting on her instincts. First she'd resigned from a job she loved and now she was getting herself involved with the last man in the world any woman in her right mind would get involved with.

So what was she supposed to do next?

She couldn't carry on nursing him, could she? She didn't trust herself.

She was going to have to leave.

She was going to have to make some excuse and—

The door slammed open with a violence that sent it crashing into the wall. Alessandro stood there, his eyes dark as a storm, one hand against the doorframe to balance himself. 'What the hell is going on, Tash? If you feel like that, why did you agree to help me?'

'Get out!' She wasn't ready to face him. *Didn't trust herself to keep him at a distance.*

'I'm not going anywhere. Not until we've had an honest conversation.'

'Honest? What do you know about honest?' It was a struggle to keep her voice even. 'One minute you—you—make a woman feel as though she's the only female alive in the world and then the next minute you—'

'The next minute I…?'

'Just forget it. I don't know why we're even talking about this. *I don't want to talk about this.*'

'We're talking about it because it's obviously on your mind. And it seems to have been on your mind for a long time.' He hobbled into the room, his jaw clenched against the pain, his muscles pumped up and hard. 'That first day in the hospital, I asked you if the past was going to be a problem and you said—'

'I know what I said.' Her voice rose. 'I don't need you to repeat it.'

His gaze was steady on hers. 'If you hate me that much, why did you agree to help me?'

'I don't hate you. I don't have any feelings for you whatsoever.' She threw out the words, knowing them to be untrue. But she badly wanted them to be true. She badly wanted to have no feelings for him. In fact, it was essential for her emotional well-being that she had no feelings for him.

'Which brings me back to the same question—why did you agree to help me?'

'Because I'd messed up my job and I was at a loose end. Because I wanted to prove that you didn't mean anything to me any more, and…' she breathed deeply '…I wanted to see if you were sorry.'

He looked at her for a long moment and then his eyes narrowed and he gave a humourless laugh. 'Ah. Now I understand. You thought you'd punish me, is that it? The strip show was for my benefit. All the "look at me" surfing sessions were designed to make me suffer. All of it was designed to make me suffer. What we shared wasn't water under the bridge. You weren't indifferent. You were getting revenge.'

'It wasn't revenge.' Tasha felt her face grow scarlet as she defended herself. 'I wanted to prove to myself that you were nothing more than a childish crush. The way I felt about you back then was— Actually, I don't even want to think about it. It's just too embarrassing. And, yes, I was angry with you. You behaved like a complete and utter bastard.'

'I know.'

'And then you—' His words penetrated her brain and she broke off and stared at him. 'What did you say?'

'I said I know. I know I treated you horribly.'

'Y-You do?' Stunned by his blunt admission, she stared at him. 'You knew that?'

'Of course. That's why I was so surprised when you waltzed blithely into my hospital room and offered to help me out. Frankly, I was expecting a black eye from you, not assistance.' He watched her cautiously. 'Clearly I was right to be suspicious of your motives.'

'But—' Anger shot through her. 'If you knew you'd behaved horribly, why didn't you ever say anything? You could at least have said sorry.'

'That would have defeated the purpose.'

'The purpose?' Tasha stared at him blankly. 'I don't get it.'

'The purpose was to make you hate me,' he said gently. 'If I'd apologised, it wouldn't have worked, would it?'

'You—you *wanted* me to hate you? Why?'

He gave a crooked smile. 'Because every time I walked into a room you looked at me as though I was the only person there. Because you thought you were in love with me. You were crazy about me, and—'

'All right, all right.' She held up her hand like a stop sign. 'Can this get any more embarrassing? Enough! I know exactly how I behaved. There's no need to rub it in.'

'I was going to say, "and I was crazy about you".' He spoke the words so softly she wondered if she'd misheard.

'You—'

'I'd never been with anyone who behaved as normally around me as you did.'

'I hero-worshiped you.'

'I know, and that was sweet, but the best part was that you were such fun. You were so unself-conscious. The first time I visited you kept trying to remember to call me Your Highness and then you just gave up and called me Sandro, and you were the first person who had ever done that. And you were so beautiful…' He shifted position awkwardly, unconsciously trying to ease the pain. 'Too beautiful. Josh introduced you as his kid sister but it didn't take me long to realise you weren't a kid. Especially when you wore those bikinis.'

Tasha watched him, her heart thumping. 'I wanted you to notice me.'

The corners of his mouth flickered. 'I noticed you.'

'And then there was the ballgown.'

'I wondered when we were going to talk about that. That night at the ball—' his eyes glittered '—I couldn't believe Josh had agreed to take you.

The only way I'd kept my distance was because I kept telling myself you were a kid. And Josh kept telling me you were a kid. And then suddenly you were standing there in this scarlet dress that made you look like a sex goddess—'

'You remember what I was wearing?'

'And suddenly telling myself that you were a kid didn't seem to be working.' His eyes were very dark. 'It didn't help that you were so wildly determined to lose your virginity that night. To me.'

Mortified at the memory of how brazen she'd been, Tasha covered her face with her hands. 'Do we have to talk about this? Isn't there just a nice deep hole I can jump into?'

'I wanted you, too.'

'Oh, sure.' Still cringing, she shook her head. 'Which is why you kissed me senseless and…' *He'd touched her,* she remembered. *Everywhere.* The memory sent fiery heat streaking through her. 'And then you walked away.'

'And why do you think I walked away, Tash?'

His intimate use of her name made her heart thud. 'Because you discovered I was flat-chested? Because I had no idea what I was doing?' His skill had left her trembling and boneless whereas she'd fumbled awkwardly, unsure of herself and of him.

'I stopped because it was the right thing to do, and that is probably the only time in my life I've done the right thing, so you should be grateful, not angry,' he confessed in a raw tone. 'I didn't know if you were a child or a woman. Damn it, I went into your bedroom to give you a message one day and your bed was covered in stuffed toys! One minute you were doing your homework, the next you were wearing a tight red dress designed to drive a man out of his mind. I wanted—well, never mind what I wanted. But I knew I had to do something drastic. That night of the ball I'd promised myself I was going to behave like a real prince. I was going to dance with you and not do anything else. But then we went out to the garden to get some fresh air and the next minute—'

'You don't need to spell it out.'

'Believe me, walking away without looking back was the hardest thing I've ever had to do. And for what it's worth, I'm sorry I hurt you, but at the time I couldn't see any other way. I wanted you to hate me.'

'You could have just told me you weren't interested.'

'I was interested. There was a chemistry between us I'd never experienced before. It was crazy, and—' He broke off. 'You were seventeen. Apart from anything else, it was barely legal.'

A warm glow burned low in her stomach. *He'd wanted her, too.* Tasha wrapped her arms around herself. 'Plenty of people have sex at seventeen.'

'You had your head in the clouds and your eyes on the stars. You were still more of a child than a woman and I had no idea how to handle someone like you. The women I mixed with were usually my age or older—heiresses, society princesses who'd been fed cynicism and experience with baby milk. You were different.'

'And it didn't occur to you to have that conversation with me?' Tasha swung her legs off the bed and stalked over to him, her eyes boring into his. 'I had a brain, Sandro. And a mind of my own.'

'I did the decent thing.'

'*Decent?* You broke my heart, Sandro. You...' She spread her hands, appalled. 'What the hell is decent about making a girl feel totally rubbish about herself? Please tell me that.'

'I didn't make you feel rubbish. I saved you from making a big mistake.'

'*Saved* me? Do you think you could have "saved" me before you ripped off my red dress?' Her face was scarlet at the memory. *The humili-*

ation. 'Then when I was totally vulnerable and ready to trust you with anything and everything, you suddenly backed away and told me to come back when I'd grown a chest. But that wasn't the worst of it. The worst of it wasn't struggling to get my ballgown back on so that a bunch of strangers didn't see me naked—and you broke the zip, by the way, so I never actually managed to get it back on—the worst was when you walked away from me straight into the arms of a tall, skinny blonde. When you kissed her I thought I was going to die.' It was good to remind herself what had happened, she thought grimly. Good to remind herself why she wasn't going to be seduced by the chemistry again.

'Tasha—'

'You knew I was watching, didn't you? At the time I assumed you didn't know I was still there, but now I see you did it for my benefit. You *wanted* me to see you kiss her.'

There was a stillness about him. A hardness about his eyes that she hadn't seen before. 'I've told you—I wanted you to hate me and forget about me. You were a kid.'

'Did I feel like a kid when you stripped me naked?'

'What do you think would have happened if I'd

taken you that night?' His tone savage, he took her chin in his fingers and lifted her face to his. 'Think.'

'We would have made love,' she whispered. 'You would have been the first.'

His fingers tightened on her face. For a moment they stared at each other, sharing the memories through that single look. 'I would have broken your heart.'

The air dragged through her lungs and each beat of her heart felt painful. 'You did that anyway. But I should be grateful. Because of you I buried myself in my books. I gave up on men.'

'That's not what I heard.' His eyes were fixed on hers, his breathing heavy. 'Josh told me you were engaged once—'

Great. More humiliation. 'That didn't work out.' Trying not to think about the fact he'd obviously discussed her with Josh, Tasha pulled away from him. 'I'm not great with relationships. I'm the first to admit it.'

'That makes two of us.'

'You have endless relationships. I read about them all the time in the paper.'

'Those aren't relationships.'

'Right.'

'For what it's worth, I'm sorry I hurt you, Tash.

I should have handled it a different way.' He adjusted his balance. 'Forgive me?'

'No! I don't forgive you.'

He was standing close to her. 'There's always been something between us and it hasn't gone away.'

'I'm older and wiser now.'

'You're still the same Tasha,' he breathed. 'Feisty, emotional, warm, giving—'

'Be quiet. I don't trust you when you're nice.'

'I'm always nice, *tesoro*.' His soft, velvety voice wrapped itself around her senses and she felt her willpower crumble.

'I'm still really angry with you,' she choked. 'I'm always going to be angry with you.'

'Even if I say sorry? *Mi dispiace.*'

She felt the warmth of his hand against her head and the heat of his body close to hers. He was a breath away from kissing her again and her eyes closed.

'No, Alessandro—please don't…' There was a tense silence and all she could hear was the sound of her own breathing. 'I mean it—I don't want you to touch me.'

For a moment she thought he was going to ignore her and then she felt his hand drop and he moved away. 'All right.' His voice was hoarse. 'I won't touch you until you ask me to.'

Disappointment mingled with relief, and the confusion of it infuriated her.

It wasn't logical to be disappointed when she was the one who'd asked him to move away.

'That will be never.' Tasha opened her eyes and looked at him, feeling as though the whole centre of her balance had shifted. 'I'd better find you another nurse.'

'Why? Last time I looked my leg was still in a cast and my ribs were still bruised.'

'I don't think I can do this,' she said desperately. 'I thought it would be easy, but it isn't. We're— You're…'

He was still standing close to her. The warmth of him, the scent of him, wound itself around her insides and sent anticipation skittering through her.

She swayed towards him and then she saw the dangerous burn of heat in his dark eyes and remembered how long it had taken her to recover last time she'd fallen for this man.

She was hopeless at relationships, wasn't she? She didn't want one. She had a career she loved. And she had to concentrate on sorting out the mess she'd made of her professional life.

'You hurt me, Alessandro.' Tasha forced the words past her lips. 'I have more self-respect than to let you do it again. I'll stay and look after you because I gave my word, but it's not going to be any more than that.'

'We thought maybe a carefully placed interview with a celebrity magazine, Your Highness, focusing on your hopes for the future...'

As his advisers droned on, Alessandro stared out of the window towards the waves. It was early morning and there was only one surfer in the waves.

Tasha. She was out there again, enjoying the swell beneath her board and the spray on her face.

Seeking distraction...

It had been three days since their conversation and she'd kept their interaction on a strictly professional level, but that didn't alter the tension that added an edge to the atmosphere whenever they were in a room together.

'Your Highness?'

Alessandro dragged his gaze from contemplation of the surfer. 'Sorry?'

His advisers exchanged glances. 'We were suggesting ways in which you could potentially raise your profile even though you're...' one of them cleared his throat and looked at Alessandro's leg '...incapacitated.'

'Featuring in a celebrity magazine?' Alessandro didn't bother to conceal his contempt for the idea. 'I don't think so.'

'It would be—'

'Shallow and useless,' Alessandro snapped. 'I don't want to be portrayed as some royal layabout. I run a successful multimillion-dollar business.' Or he had until his brother's death. Now a select team ran it in his place and he was only involved in the major decisions.

'The important thing is that the people want to see *you*, Your Highness. They want to know their prince. They'll pay an enormous sum for the interview.' His chief adviser named a figure that made Alessandro shake his head in disbelief.

'They'll pay that much to take pictures of me lying on the sofa with my leg in plaster? The world has gone mad.'

'The money would be given to your favourite charity, Your Highness, and that would be excellent publicity.'

'And both contrived and manipulative.' Alessandro felt bitter distaste for the workings of the media. 'If they have that kind of money to throw around then let them just donate it to the charity in the first place. Cut out the middle man.'

'Her Highness, the Princess Eleanor wants—'

'I know what my mother wants.' His tone cold, Alessandro stared at the thick file they'd brought with them. 'What do you have there?'

'We've outlined proposals for various ways of supporting charity and generally raising your profile in these…' the man's hands trembled slightly as he pushed the file across the table '… difficult and limiting circumstances. The ideas have been approved by the palace. The one that Her Highness particularly wanted us to draw your attention to is—' He broke off, a sheen of sweat on his brow.

'Is?' Alessandro's silken prompt made the man flinch.

'Is the suggestion that you announce your engagement, sir.'

It was like being caught in an avalanche. The cold slammed into him, suffocating him and chilling him right to the bone.

When he didn't speak, the man cleared his throat. 'It's been a while, Your Highness, and everyone assumes—'

'I know what everyone assumes.' Alessandro barely recognised his own voice. He leaned back against the sofa, suddenly exhausted. 'Leave the file. I'll read it and tell you what I intend to do.'

'Yes, Your Highness.'

They left and Alessandro stayed where he was. The file remained unopened.

The thought of allowing sycophantic journalists and photographers into his private life made him cold inside. But the thing that made him coldest of all was the prospect of announcing his engagement. The last thing he wanted was marriage. Given the choice he would have stayed single rather than risk the sort of relationship his parents had. But he didn't have the choice, did he? It was up to him to produce the next generation to rule the Mediterranean island of San Savarre. It didn't matter whether he liked it or not.

Filling his brother's shoes.

He needed to talk to Miranda. He needed to *see* Miranda. But instead of seeing Miranda's sleek blonde hair and elegant clothes, he saw Tasha putting chilli in his food, undaunted by royal protocol. *Hope I'm not supposed to bow or curtsey.*

Tasha, walking away from him.

Since their heated, tense exchange they had hardly seen each other and Alessandro knew that she was staying out in the surf as long as possible to avoid him.

Telling himself that it was probably a good thing, Alessandro hobbled through to the bedroom and turned on the television in the hope of distraction.

By the time she arrived back from her session in the waves, he'd pulled himself together and he focused hard on the screen as she whirled through the apartment like a tornado, singing to herself as if nothing had happened between them.

Alessandro watched her steadily. *She was putting on an act.*

'Hi, there, hopalong!' she called to him as she stripped off the jacket she'd put on over her wetsuit and walked jauntily towards her bedroom. 'Surf's up today and this time I'm not saying that to make you want to thump me.'

'Tasha—'

'Need to get out of my wet things!'

He had to admire her performance. If he hadn't known better he would have said she was indifferent. But he knew she was far from indifferent. Watching her breeze through the house, he wondered how long she was going to keep up the pretence that nothing was happening between them. 'When I finally get this damn plaster off my leg, I'll join you.' They were going through the motions. Talking about surfing, even though that wasn't the topic uppermost in their thoughts.

He heard the soft hiss of water as she turned on the shower and immediately he started thinking about Tasha naked. And thinking about Tasha naked—

Cursing softly, he picked up the remote control and flicked on the sports channel.

'How did your meeting go?' She was standing in the doorway, wearing a T-shirt and a pair of shorts. Her hair was still wet from the shower and her feet bare. 'What do they want you to do?'

Get married.

'The usual stuff. Palace promotion. I'm afraid I'm not very good at being told what to do. I've always been a bit of a rebel that way. Antonio was the dutiful one. He was the Good Son.' He felt the bed give as she sat down next to him.

'You must miss him terribly. I know you were close.' Her voice was soft and for the time being she seemed to have abandoned her act. 'I can't begin to imagine how I'd cope if I lost a brother.'

'We both had our roles. I was the bad boy. Even as kids it was the same. It never occurred to me I'd have to play his role. The truth is, I'm not good at it. No matter how much my parents would like me to be, I'm not my brother.'

Alessandro wondered why he was telling her this. He never talked about it. Not to anyone.

But talking to Tasha had always been easy. She had a way of making a person spill the contents of their minds.

'No, you're not your brother. You're you, an individual.' She hesitated. 'I suppose you have to find a way to do it that suits you. A way you're OK with. I mean, Josh and I are both doctors but we're not the same. We don't approach things the same way. He's very analytical whereas I'm more emotional. But I don't think either one of us is better or worse than the other. We're just different.'

'The problem is, my parents don't want different. If they could have chosen, I would have been the one who died in that car.'

'Don't say that.' She sounded shocked and then her forehead creased into a tiny frown. 'The other night when we were talking—you said it was your fault...'

Had he said that to her? 'Forget it.'

'But—'

'If you want to help me, you can fetch that big fat file from the table in the living room.' Alessandro gave a humourless laugh. 'I have to go through it and pick out which duties I'm up to performing. I need to kiss some babies in public.'

And he needed to finally announce his engagement.

'Kiss babies? Sounds like a recipe for disease transmission to me. I'll warn infection control. Now, lie back and let me take a look at your ribs to see how quickly you're healing. It will give me some idea of what you're capable of doing. It's no good opening a hospital and then finding yourself as a patient.'

Remembering what had happened the last time she'd touched him, Alessandro's eyes narrowed warily. 'No need. I'm fine.'

'I'm the one who's going to tell you if you're fine.' She pushed him back with the palm of her hand. 'And wipe that look off your face. I'm in doctor mode. I don't think about sex when I'm in doctor mode. And, anyway, I told you I'm not interested.' Ignoring his protests, she unbuttoned his shirt with brisk fingers. The fact that there was nothing lover-like about her expression did nothing to lessen his libido.

'What about the patient?' Alessandro gritted his teeth. 'What if the patient starts thinking about sex?'

'That would be seriously perverted. After all,

I'm hurting you. The bruising is better.' Frowning, she trailed her fingers lightly over his chest. 'Does this hurt?'

'It depends which part of me you're asking about.'

'Don't be disgusting. This is why I chose to be a children's doctor.' But her voice was mild as she slid her fingers up to his shoulders and pressed. 'Does this hurt?'

'If I say yes, will you stop?'

'It obviously doesn't hurt as much as before because you're not doing that clenched-teeth thing. I think you're definitely on the mend.'

'Good, then can we—?'

'I just want to listen to your breath sounds.' She'd left her stethoscope on the table by his bed and as she reached for it her hair tumbled forward, brushing over his arm. 'I'm just going to—'

'So am I.' Driven past the point of control, Alessandro cupped her face in his hands and brought her mouth down on his. Her lips opened under his and he tasted shock mingled with sweetness. For a moment he thought she was going to pull away, but as his tongue slid against hers he felt her moan and tighten her grip on his shoulders. There was a delicious inevitability to the kiss that simply added to the excitement. It was the culmination of the tension and anticipation that had been building between them since the morning she'd walked into his hospital room.

Apparently forgetting all her protests about not wanting him to touch her, Tasha ripped at his shirt, hesitating as he gave a grunt of pain when her fingers made contact with bruised flesh. 'Sorry…' She panted the word against his mouth and pulled back but he grabbed her, his fingers hard on her arms.

'Don't stop. For God's sake, don't stop,' he groaned, his mind at war with his senses. 'Do you want to stop? You didn't want to do this—'

'Changed my mind—' Their mouths clashed, the kiss exciting and erotic, and he rolled her onto her back and then swore fluently as pain overtook him.

'This is—'

'A challenge. I have a better idea.' Desperate, she pushed him back gently and straddled him, her hair falling forward, brushing his bare chest. Her eyes were like dark, dangerous pools. 'I'm the one in charge. If I hurt you, tell me.'

'I think that's supposed to be my line.' Alessandro pulled her head down to his and took her mouth with explicit intent, tasting sweetness and a desperation that matched his.

'God, you're beautiful.' He groaned the words against her lips. 'How did I keep my hands off you all those years ago?'

'You didn't.' Frantic, she tore at his clothes and he tore at hers until only flimsy underwear separated them.

Panting, breathless, they kissed like two crazy people. They were so wrapped up in each other that they were oblivious to anything but the heat they were creating. Which was why they didn't hear the sound in the distance.

'Tasha? Alessandro? Anyone there?' Josh's voice came from the living room of the house and Tasha froze as if she'd been shot. Her eyes flew open and she dragged her mouth from the seductive pressure of his.

'Ohmigod!'

'Oops.' Hiding his frustration, Alessandro gave her a crooked smile and stroked her hair back from her face. 'It's your brother. That's not great timing. You might want to put your clothes on, *tesoro*. I don't want him to see you naked.'

CHAPTER SIX

'THIS is *all* your fault! I told you not to kiss me.' Tasha yanked her top back over her head and freed her hair. 'Stay there. You're not safe to be around. I was in doctor mode. How the hell did we end up naked?'

'Because the chemistry doesn't go away just because you're clutching a stethoscope. I want you, Tasha. Make no mistake about that.' His smooth, possessive declaration stopped her breathing. For an injured man he was far too threatening.

'I…' confused, she tumbled off the bed, grabbing her clothes. Glancing briefly at him, she collided with dark, burning eyes and felt her insides melt. 'No.' It was both a plea and a protest. 'Just—no.'

She'd promised herself that she wasn't going to do this. That she wasn't going to fall under his spell again.

She was a career-woman. She had a five-year plan and it didn't include falling for a wicked, sexy prince. She'd had herself under control. She'd been doing really well.

Until he'd kissed her...

'Damn you, Sandro. I need to get dressed before he comes looking for us.' Her face burning, Tasha grabbed the rest of her clothes, desperately conscious of those coal-black eyes following her every move. The heat was still in the room, simmering between them like a blast from the sun.

If he was bothered by the fact that her brother was in his house, he didn't show it. But Alessandro wasn't the sort to run from anything, she knew that. In fact, that was part of the problem. He had too much of the devil in him.

And that devil had drawn her just as it had when she was a teenager.

In her haste to drag on her clothes, Tasha couldn't untangle her jeans and they were halfway up her legs when her brother tapped on the door and opened it.

Tasha gave a whimper of horror. She didn't know which was worse—her brother seeing her semi-naked, or her brother seeing her semi-naked with Alessandro.

'Hey, you guys—I thought I'd drop by and see

if you've killed each other yet…' His voice faded as he saw them and for a moment Tasha stared like a rabbit at oncoming headlights.

Oh, dear…

'Hi, Josh.' Hands shaking, she finally managed to zip her jeans. She felt as mortified as she had when Josh had caught her kissing the captain of the football team when she was sixteen. 'We weren't expecting you.' She tried to sound casual, as if dressing in Alessandro's room was an everyday occurrence. With any luck Josh would decide to turn a blind eye.

But one look at the flat, disapproving line of her brother's mouth told her this wasn't going to be her lucky day.

'What the hell are you doing?' Josh's voice was tight and the shock in his eyes turned dark as approaching storm clouds as he turned his gaze on Alessandro, who stared right back at him.

'Seducing your sister. If you have a problem with that, take it out on me, not her.'

'You—' Josh was across the room in a flash and Tasha hastily planted herself in front of Alessandro.

'No!' Her legs were shaking and she was mortified at being caught kissing, but most of all she was mortified that she'd been kissing Alessandro in the first place.

That definitely hadn't been part of the master plan.

'Josh, calm down! It's nothing to get into a sweat over.' Actually, it was, but the sweating was going to have to wait for another time because at the moment her brother looked dangerous and she felt a twinge of real fear.

'Calm down? *Calm down?*' Josh closed his hands over her arms and moved her bodily to one side, his voice thick with anger as he confronted his friend. 'I arrange for my sister to nurse you and this is how you repay me?'

Tasha bristled. 'Excuse me! I do have a mind of my own, you know. You might have been the one who suggested it, but—'

'Shut up, Tasha.' Josh growled the words. 'This isn't your business.'

Alessandro shifted his leg. 'It certainly isn't yours, my friend.'

He should have looked vulnerable, but he didn't. In fact, somehow he managed to look physically intimidating, even with broken bones and bruised ribs, Tasha thought absently. She wondered whether his natural air of command was something to do with being royalty or whether it was just the man.

Warrior Prince.

Josh was red in the face. 'It has everything to do with me. She's my sister!'

Tasha opened her mouth to protest again and realised that neither man was taking any notice of her.

Their eyes were fixed on each other in full combat mode. Alessandro stared Josh straight in the eye, the challenge blatant. 'And this time she's way above the age of consent. I repeat—it has nothing to do with you.'

This time? Tasha frowned at that remark but she didn't have time to dwell on it because the two men were squaring up for a fight.

Josh stepped forward, his expression ugly, his hands clenched. 'And that's all it takes for you, is it? She's old enough so that makes it OK? Well, I've got news for you, Alessandro, it doesn't make it OK. And she's leaving here right now.' Without turning his head, Josh pointed his finger at the door. 'Pack your bags, Tasha.'

Tasha raised her eyebrows, assuming he was joking. When she realised he wasn't, she put her hands on her hips and threw her head back. 'I will *not* pack my bags! Are you deranged? Listen to you!' Her own temper spilled over. 'I'm not six years old, Josh. I'm a grown woman, and if I want to kiss a man, I'll kiss him and I don't have to ask your permission first.' She vented her anger on Josh, even though she knew deep down that most of it should be directed at herself.

She'd been stupid, stupid, stupid...

'You're my sister.' His tone was raw and angry. 'Don't argue with me. Go and pack. This is between Allesandro and I.'

'Oh, for God's sake, will you listen to yourself? "*This is between Allessandro and I,*"' Tasha mimicked his tone. 'What are you going to do, Josh? Challenge him to a duel? Pistols at dawn? This is the twenty-first century. Get over yourself.'

'This isn't your business, Natasha.'

'Well, *excuse* me—' she emphasised each word '—but I was the one naked with him, not you. I think that makes it my business, not yours.'

Josh gave a low growl. 'You were *naked* with him?'

Yes, and she had no idea how it had happened. Clearly at some point during the burn of chemistry, her brain had disconnected itself from her body. But she didn't want to think about that right now. 'So what if I was? *What is your problem?*

You do not just barge in here and tell me what to do. Do I ask you what's happening in your love life? Do I lecture you or ask you who you got naked with last night? When I saw you coming out of that on-call room a couple of weeks ago, having had a night of hot sex, did I demand to know who was in the room with you?'

Alessandro raised an eyebrow. 'Hey, Josh, you had a night of hot sex? Good man.'

'Shut up!' Brother and sister spoke simultaneously and Tasha stabbed Josh in the chest with her finger.

'I wanted to ask who she was, but I didn't because I respect your privacy and your ability to make your own decisions. I understand that you're an adult. If you want to have a one-night stand in the on-call room, that's up to you.'

There was a tense, frozen silence.

Josh's face had turned from scarlet to grey. 'It wasn't a one-night stand. And this isn't about me, it's about you.'

'Precisely.' Tasha folded her arms and pursed her lips. 'Which makes it my business, not yours. If I want to sleep with a man, I'll sleep with him. I don't need your permission.'

Josh's shoulders sagged and suddenly he looked

exhausted. 'Fine.' His voice was brittle. 'You're right, of course. I apologise.'

Startled by the sudden change in him, Tasha frowned. One minute he was yelling at her and the next he looked as though his brain was on another planet. 'So—when I need a knight in shining armour, I'll text you.'

Alessandro started to laugh. 'I hate to break it to you, Josh, but I think your baby sister is all grown up and slaying her own dragons.'

Josh was still looking at Tasha. A tiny muscle flickered in his cheek and he shook his head slightly, as if trying to focus. 'Just as long as you know he will break your heart,' he said shakily. 'You'll fall in love, because that's what you do, and he'll smash you to pieces. I don't want that for you. I don't want you loving someone you can't be with. I wouldn't wish that on anyone.' There was an anguished note to his tone that killed Tasha's anger like water on flame.

Instinct told her there was more to her brother's words than a throw-away comment.

I don't want you loving someone you can't be with.

Suddenly she knew that his explosion of emotion was driven by something deeper than her own indiscretion. Something much more personal.

'Josh…' Her voice faltered. 'I—'

'I'm just telling you to be careful, that's all.' Cutting her dead, he blanked the emotion and walked to the door. 'I'll leave the two of you alone. I'm sorry I interrupted. And who am I to give advice on relationships? It's a subject I know nothing about.'

His departure was more painful than his arrival.

Tasha felt her heart clench. Her brother was suffering and she sensed that his anguish went much deeper than concern about her.

Was this about the woman in the on-call room?

'Wait!' Tasha sprinted after him. 'Don't just walk off—for crying out loud, Josh, will you *wait*?'

He kept walking, talking over his shoulder as he strode through Alessandro's double-height living room. 'I need breakfast. I've been working all night. I have to get back to the hospital.'

'I'll make you breakfast.' Catching up with him, she caught his arm. 'The kitchen here is like a spaceship and I can do amazing things with eggs. Please.'

'I need to be on my own.' He shook her off and

she saw the emptiness in his eyes as he detached from her. 'I'm sorry I disturbed you.'

Tasha felt a flash of exasperation but this time it was fuelled by real concern for her brother. 'It wasn't like that, Josh—honestly, it was nothing.' She didn't know what it was and she hadn't had time to work it out, but at the moment her priority was Josh. 'I want you to stay. I haven't seen you properly since I arrived. Let's chat. Catch up.'

'Sit down, Josh.' Alessandro's slightly accented drawl came from behind them. Tasha realised that while she and Josh had been arguing Alessandro had hauled himself from the bed and was now gripping the doorframe. His shirt—*the shirt she'd ripped*—hung loose around his body, exposing his bronzed muscled chest. 'I'm going mad trapped in this place. I need male conversation.'

Tasha gave a faint smile. 'Men don't have conversations. They just exchange sporting results.' But she was relieved that Alessandro had added his voice to hers.

Josh looked undecided and the look he gave Alessandro was cold. 'I should go—'

'There's a wealth of difference between what one should do and what one chooses to do,' Alessandro drawled. 'Sit down. Your sister isn't a bad cook, providing you keep her away from chilli.'

Tasha opened her mouth and closed it again. This wasn't the time to give him a lecture on the emancipation of women.

Josh relaxed slightly. 'Are you going to promise not to touch my sister again?'

'No.' Alessandro's tone was calm and he lifted his hand as Josh's eyes flared. 'But I promise to stop if she asks me to. Fair enough?'

Josh's mouth was a tight line. 'I don't think—'

'Hello? I'm over here!' Exasperated, Tasha waved at both of them. 'You don't need to talk about me as if I don't exist. In fact, you don't need to talk about me at all. Let's just drop the whole subject.' She was relieved to see her brother sprawl on the deep leather sofa.

As he ran his hand over his face she realised that he hadn't slept in a long time.

The sunlight pouring through the floor-to-ceiling windows simply accentuated the shadows under his eyes and the pallor of his skin. Why had it taken her so long to notice how awful he looked?

Because she'd been too busy getting her clothes on.

'So...' She sank down on the sofa next to him

and curled her legs underneath her. 'You look wrecked.'

'Thanks.'

'Have you been working nights or something?' Even as she asked the question, she dismissed it. Josh never had any trouble coping with work volume, so it couldn't be that. Which meant it must be a woman. But the split with Rebecca had been mutual…

Using a process of elimination, she mentally ticked off the options and decided that it had to be something to do with the woman he'd had in the on-call room.

She'd thought at the time that he was behaving oddly.

Suddenly she wished she could send Alessandro into the kitchen so that she could question her brother in private.

'So how's the leg?' His expression slightly less black, Josh looked at his oldest friend. 'Are you healing?'

'Yes, but not fast enough.' Alessandro limped over to the other sofa and sat down. He'd mastered the art of keeping his movements as smooth as possible to reduce jarring. 'I'm hoping this cast will be off soon, then I can get back to normal duties.'

'Palace giving you a hard time?'

'They are not amused,' Alessandro said lightly, a sardonic smile on his face. 'I'm supposed to be earning my keep, not "lounging" around here.'

'You can't do much with your leg like that.' Josh's gaze flickered to Tasha. 'Except mess with my sister.'

'Let's not go there again.' Alessandro leaned back against the sofa. His shirt flopped open, revealing smooth bronzed skin and well-defined muscle. Feeling suddenly dizzy, Tasha was about to tell him to button it up when she realised that he couldn't because she'd ripped the buttons.

Concern for her brother mingled with the realisation that the chemistry between her and Alessandro was as powerful as ever.

So much for the childish crush theory. So much for proving to him that she was indifferent.

Satisfied that they weren't going to kill each other, Tasha used the excuse of breakfast to escape to the kitchen.

Behind the safety of the closed door, she took refuge in mindless cooking to keep her mind off Alessandro. She didn't want to think about Alessandro. She wanted to know what was wrong with Josh.

People said women were complicated, but at

least women usually talked about their problems. Frustrated and grumpy, she chopped fruit into a bowl and then remembered she was feeding men and fried a stack of bacon.

Walking back into the living room with a heaped tray, she found the two men deep in conversation about sport. The earlier argument might never have happened.

They were lifelong friends, of course, and the bond showed as they talked easily, barely acknowledging Tasha as she deposited the tray on the table.

'Hello? Earth to Neanderthals,' she said cheerfully. 'I've cooked it, but I draw the line at actually forking the food into your mouths. That bit you can manage yourselves if you really concentrate.'

'Thanks, Tasha.' Josh sat forward and helped himself to bacon. 'I can't be long. They're holding a prince-and-princess party on the children's ward this afternoon and I promised to dress up as a prince. Which means I have a pile of work to get finished this morning.'

Tasha felt her insides tighten at the mention of the children's ward. She missed it dreadfully.

Being with Alessandro had distracted her slightly from her life, but now reality was back

with full force. What if she couldn't find another job? What if she'd messed everything up
for good?

Oblivious to her anxieties, Alessandro was
laughing at Josh. 'You trained for all those years
to pretend to be a prince?'

'It isn't funny. I should have said no.'

'So why didn't you?'

He hesitated. 'Because a friend asked me.
There are some kids who have been on the unit
for ages—they're bored and need some distraction.' Josh bit into his sandwich. 'Someone came
up with the idea of having a prince-and-princess
tea party so that they can dress up. Tiaras—that
sort of thing. Because I'm not officially working
today, I'm supposed to arrive halfway through
dressed as Prince Charming.'

Tasha slid her hands round her mug of tea.
'You're kidding.'

'I did Father Christmas last year.' Josh wiped
his fingers on a napkin. 'What's the difference?'

'Is that a serious question?' Alessandro was
still laughing. 'One is fat and wears a red coat.
The other is suave and capable of slaying dragons.'

Tasha sat with the mug halfway to her mouth,

watching the way Alessandro's eyes shone and his cheeks creased when he laughed.

He was the sexiest man she'd ever met.

It was just as well Josh couldn't read her mind.

'No dragons at our tea party. This bacon is good, Tasha. I can't remember when you last cooked for me. Usually you glare at me and tell me it's not women's work. Are you all right?' Josh frowned at his sister. 'Why are you staring at Alessandro?'

'I'm keeping an eye on his colour,' she said smoothly. 'If he does too much, he gets tired.'

'He didn't look that tired when I arrived.' His tone dry, Josh helped himself to more bacon. 'He looked as though he had all his faculties. He won't need you for much longer.'

Tasha wondered if her brother was having another dig. 'I'll stay until he's able to cope without help.'

'Have you applied for any jobs?'

Tasha leaned forward and stacked the plates. 'Not yet.'

'Why not?'

'Because I don't know what I'd say in the interview about why I left my last job. I'm worried everyone is going to think I'm a troublemaker.' Tasha rescued the ketchup before it could tumble onto the floor. 'I miss medicine. I miss the kids. I miss being part of a unit. I miss—all of it. I'm a doctor. I want patients.' Aware that Alessandro was no longer smiling, she suddenly wished she hadn't said anything. 'Sorry, it's just that I had this great career plan and then—*poof*—I managed to blow the whole thing. Well done, Tasha.' She knew that her light tone hadn't fooled them. 'Anyway, I don't know why we're talking about me. I already have a job for the time being. Preventing Alessandro from trying to run before he can walk.'

'I can tell you're a paediatric doctor. You're treating me like a kid.'

He wasn't a kid at all. He was a grown man and she was horribly aware of every bronzed, handsome inch of him. She'd thought her anger would keep her safe, but her anger had vanished. She'd thought her feelings were all from the past. But the explosion of passion that had erupted between them had nothing to do with the past and everything to do with the present.

Fear flashed through her. If she let him, he'd hurt her again. Just as he had the first time. And she wasn't going to let a man do that to her…

The sooner she found herself a paediatric job, the better.

'You shouldn't feel insecure. You're a good doctor, Tasha.' Josh stole the last piece of bacon. 'Remember that little girl you saw on the unit that day you came to my office to tell me you'd resigned? Turned out you were right. It wasn't hay fever. She had a congenital heart defect.'

Alessandro looked bemused. 'I didn't think Tasha worked on your unit.'

'She doesn't. But she walked past this girl and saw something that none of my doctors had seen.' Josh gave a smile. 'She's very intuitive, my baby sister.'

Snapping out of her dream, Tasha stared at him. 'The girl had a congenital heart defect? You're sure?'

'She's already seen the cardiologist. You probably saved her life.'

'Oh.' She felt an ache of sympathy for the child and the mother. 'I wish it had just been hay fever. Poor little thing.' Suddenly she missed her job even more. She wanted to be the one looking after the child, supporting her and helping her through a difficult time. She could make a difference, she knew she could.

'This prince-and-princess party…' Alessandro eased his leg into a more comfortable position. 'That must be something I can help with.'

Josh glanced at him with a frown. 'You?'

'You should be saving lives, not dressing up as a prince. I don't have your medical skills, but I can do the prince bit.' His tone was loaded with irony. 'I've never dressed up in a cloak or worn a crown, but if it would help the kids I can do it. Provided someone keeps the paparazzi at a distance. I'm doing it for the children, not the press.'

'Why keep them at a distance?' Tasha jumped to her feet. 'It's a brilliant idea. Your mother wants some good publicity—what better than the prince visiting the children's ward? You can autograph stuff for them. They can have pictures taken with you. They'd love that. I'll come with you.' Better to be on the children's ward as a visitor than not be there at all, she reasoned.

'How far from the car to the ward? I can't walk that far on this damn leg of mine.'

Tasha opened her mouth to suggest a wheel-chair but took one look at the set of his jaw and closed her mouth again. Alessandro would drag himself across the ground by his fingernails before he'd agree to use a wheelchair.

'It's a great idea. We can drop you right outside. And Tasha can come with you.' Josh nodded. 'I'll have a word with the staff and let them know you're coming.'

'I've been thinking about a job in NICU. Is there someone there I could talk to?'

Alessandro frowned. 'What's NICU?'

'Neonatal intensive care unit.' Josh shifted in his chair. 'Talk to Megan Phillips.'

Tasha noticed that her brother's tone had altered and wondered if it had anything to do with Megan. Glancing up, she met Alessandro's steady dark gaze. Clearly he was thinking the same thing. He smiled and that slow, sexy smile connected straight to her insides. Her stomach swooped and plunged, the chemistry between them as electrifying and terrifying as ever. Staring into his mahogany eyes, she opened her mouth to speak but he spoke first.

'You've got me through the worst bit. Thanks to you, they let me out of that hospital. I can manage now. If you want to leave, leave.'

He was giving her a choice. And she knew it wasn't just about caring for him.

He was making her decide whether to leave or not.

Both men were looking at her expectantly and Tasha swallowed. She didn't know how she was going to answer until the words left her mouth.

'I'm not in the habit of letting people down. I'll stay until you're fully mobile, just as I promised.' It was easy to convince herself that that was the reason she was staying. 'But I do need to be looking for a full-time job. I thought I'd explore NICU—except that I'm not sure I'll get a reference.'

'You will. I made a few phone calls this week.' Josh leaned back against the sofa. 'Turns out you had a lot of support at the unit. Questions are being asked. People are enraged that you were allowed to resign.'

'Really? Why didn't you say so before?' Tasha brightened. 'Enraged? Oh, I'm so pleased.'

Alessandro lifted an eyebrow. 'You want people to be enraged?'

'I want them to care that I've gone, yes. I'm human enough to want that. And I'm human enough to need to be told I did the right thing— that others would have done the same. I would love an apology from him,' she sniffed, 'but I doubt I'll get that.'

'You won't. They guy's an idiot. Forget about him.' Josh leaned forward. 'So, about the prince-and-princess party…'

Energised by the knowledge that people were supporting her, Tasha reached for her handbag.

'Leave that to me. I'm going to pay a visit to the dressing-up shop in St Piran. Alessandro and I will see you back at the hospital.'

He'd given her the opportunity to leave and yet she'd chosen to stay.

Alessandro watched Tasha as she gathered bags and put them in the car. Her coat was buttoned from neck to hem and he wondered why she was wearing a long coat when it wasn't cold.

'I've bought tiaras and all sorts of props that should be useful.' She slid his crutches into the boot. 'Be careful as you get in. Sit down, then I'll move your legs.'

She gently moved his leg into the car and helped him with his seat belt. 'Is that comfortable?'

It was agony, but even agony wasn't enough to dampen his response to her.

'Alessandro?' She lifted her eyes to his face and chemistry immediately flickered between them. Flushing, she drew back sharply. 'Right. Well, if you're not too uncomfortable then we'll get going.'

'Tasha, listen—'

'The kids are waiting.' The car door slammed and Alessandro winced as pain rocked through his leg. Fine. So they'd go through the day pretending they hadn't stripped each other half-naked.

'Did you agree to stay with me just to annoy your brother?' He watched her as she slid into the driver's seat. 'If you want to take a job at the hospital, you should take it. I can manage.'

'I promised to look after you until you're out of the cast and that's what I'm going to do. And, anyway, I don't really want to work in the same hospital as Josh. You've seen what he's like. He'll be banging on my door, questioning every decision I make. We'd drive each other crazy.' She drove fast and Alessandro found himself clenching his teeth.

'Do you know these roads well?'

'Yes.'

'Good, because if there are any surprises behind that blind bend, you're about to smack into it head first.'

She shifted gears smoothly. 'Do I make you nervous? Big, tough guy like you?'

An image of tangled metal lodged itself in his head. 'I'm not a good passenger.' He didn't elaborate but she immediately trod on the brakes.

'Sorry,' she muttered. 'I didn't think.'

Her sensitivity surprised him, although it

shouldn't have. She'd always been sensitive, hadn't she? *Too sensitive.*

He braced himself for her to question him about the accident that had killed his brother but instead she smoothly changed the subject.

'Did you notice anything strange about Josh?'

'Strange in what way?'

'You didn't think he was tense and on edge?'

'He'd just caught his sister naked with a man.' He watched as the colour bloomed in her cheeks. 'That was reason enough for him to be tense.'

'Yes, but it wasn't that. It was something else. Something personal. Did you see his face when he made that little speech about loving someone you couldn't be with?'

'He's worried about you.'

'I'm not sixteen years old.' This time her gear change was vicious. 'Why do men always think a woman has to be in love? This is the twenty-first century. I don't want love. The most important thing to me is my career. And, anyway, a woman can have sex without being in love.' The words spilled out of her and he watched her steadily, wondering why he wasn't convinced.

'We didn't have sex, Tasha.'

The gears crunched again. 'I'm well aware of that. All I'm saying is that if we *had* had sex then it wouldn't have had anything to do with being in love, and I can't imagine why you'd even think that. Women can have sex like a man. Without emotional involvement. I don't want emotional involvement.'

'Right.' Alessandro tried to imagine Tasha doing anything without emotional involvement, and failed. Her emotions were involved in everything, from cooking chilli to handling her stethoscope. 'So, if that's the case, why are you worried about what Josh said?'

'There's something wrong with him. He's been acting really strangely since I caught him in the on-call room that day I came to see you...' Without breaking the conversation she flicked the indicator and turned into the hospital car park. 'And I know he had someone in the room with him, but he was hiding the fact. He didn't want me to know. But when I saw him, he looked all lit up inside. As if something special had happened. There was an energy about him that I haven't seen for years.'

'So maybe he's found someone. What's wrong with that?'

'Nothing. But today he didn't look like that. He looked exhausted.' She pulled into a parking space and gnawed at her lower lip with her teeth. 'He looked awful, Sandro.'

'He works hard.'

'I know, but he always has. Josh has endless reserves when it comes to work. It's something else. Something to do with a woman, I'm sure of it.'

Looking at her troubled expression, Alessandro wondered why it was that women had to analyse everything in such depth. 'Maybe he's met some-one and she's married.'

'Josh would never have an affair with a married woman.'

'He was married himself. Still is, isn't he?'

'His relationship with Rebecca has been dead for ages.'

Alessandro felt the cold trickle down his spine. 'That's what marriage does to people.'

'Do you really believe that?'

'How many happy marriages have you seen?'

She hesitated. 'Just because we haven't seen them, it doesn't mean they don't exist.'

'Does it matter? I thought you said you could have sex without emotional involvement.'

'I can. But that doesn't mean I don't believe that happy marriages don't exist.' She snapped her seat belt and Alessandro watched her for a moment.

'If you're worried about Josh, why don't you just ask him what's wrong, instead of subjecting yourself to all this guesswork?'

'I've tried—obliquely. But he dodges it. And then this morning…' she retrieved her bag '…he just seemed really stressed about something.'

'He'd just seen you naked with me,' Alessandro drawled. He knew from past experience that was sufficient reason to stress Josh. 'In case you hadn't worked it out, your brothers are very possessive of you. Particularly Josh.'

'Maybe we should invite him round for supper so that we can chat properly. I could cook something.'

'Something with chilli?'

She grinned wickedly. 'I don't know how you ate that.'

'The eating it was fine. It was putting out the fire afterwards that was the problem.' Alessandro eased his leg out of the car, clenching his jaw against the pain as Tasha lifted the bags out of the boot.

As he straightened up she slung a cloak around his shoulders.

'All hail, Prince Alessandro. Welcome to the

Kingdom of Sick Child.' She curtseyed deep and he stared down at the velvet cloak in wry amusement.

'What on earth is this?'

''Tis your finest clothing, sire. Otherwise known as prince's-cape-from-dressing-up-shop.' She stood up. 'Don't you dare refuse to wear it—took me ages to track it down. There's a cute crown to go with it. They threw it in free.' As she rummaged in the bag, Alessandro glanced around the car park to check that there were no photographers.

'There is no way am I wearing a velvet cloak and a plastic crown to walk across the car park.'

'Not even for sick children? They might be watching from the window.' She batted her eyelashes but Alessandro didn't flinch.

'If they're watching from the window, they can't be that sick.'

'I just want you to make an entrance.' As she spoke she slid off her coat and Alessandro almost swallowed his tongue as he saw what she was wearing.

'What—?'

'How do you do, Your Highness? I'm the Princess Tasha.' She beamed at him and gave a quick twirl. The shimmery pink dress swirled and floated around her slender frame. Still smiling, she reached into the bag and pulled out a tiara. Ducking down to look in the wing mirror, Tasha slid it into her hair and adjusted it. 'Just need to fit the crown jewels. There. Perfect. How do I look?'

Alessandro ran his tongue over his lips, grateful for the cloak.

When he didn't reply, she frowned at him. 'Do I look like a princess?'

'No.' His voice came out as a hoarse croak. 'At least, you don't look anything like the ones I've met.' And he'd met a few. *Too many.*

Her face fell and she took another sneaky look in the mirror. 'I thought I looked cute.'

'You do look cute. But princesses don't generally look cute. In my experience they're usually hard and cynical.' He gave a crooked smile. 'Comes from having contact with too many wicked princes, I guess.'

'See? *That's* why I'd never want to be a princess. If I can't be the fantasy version, I'm not interested.'

He loved her energy and her sense of fun.

He loved the fact that she treated him the same way she treated everyone else.

Alessandro dragged his eyes away from the

twist of hair that had come loose from the tiara
and decided that the sooner she went back to
work as a doctor, the better for his sanity.

He wondered what would have happened if
Josh hadn't arrived in the house when he had.
Would either of them have stopped?

'Let's go. I don't want to stand around wearing
a velvet cloak and a crown for longer than I have
to. If the press sees me, I'm never going to live
this one down.'

'You'll be accused of being typecast,' Tasha
said cheerfully, dropping the car keys into a silky
pink bag and waiting while he balanced himself.
'Do you want a hand?'

'No, I've got it.' Leaning on the crutches,
Alessandro struggled into the hospital and onto
the children's ward.

Balloons were tied in huge clusters and a red
'carpet'—a long piece of scarlet fabric—stretched
along the corridor to a brightly painted playroom.

'Welcome, Your Highness.' A nurse in a
long flowing dress swept a deep curtsey and
Alessandro was about to say something flippant
when he saw a little girl in a wheelchair, watching him with tears in her eyes.

Disconcerted, he watched her cautiously.

Great. He'd been here less than five seconds

and already he'd made someone cry. Suddenly he wished he hadn't interfered. He should have let Josh do it.

Tasha reached for his arm but he shrugged her off and limped across to the child. He'd volunteered for this so he was going to do it. Without help.

'Hey, there—that's a very pretty dress you're wearing.'

Her face turned the colour of a tomato. 'Are you a real live prince?'

'I am.'

'Is that a real crown?'

Alessandro remembered that Tasha had said you should always be honest with children so he shook his head. 'No, it's plastic. Fake. The police get jumpy if I walk around Cornwall wearing a real crown.' Seeing her face fall, he searched his brain for inspiration. 'But I do have a real one. At home.' Leaning forward, he whispered in her ear. 'If you ever visit my country, I'll give you a private tour of the state jewel collection.'

'You will?' Her eyes went huge. 'Do you have alarms and guard dogs and stuff?'

'All of that. And bodyguards.' Seeing how thin she was, Alessandro felt his heart twist. Suddenly he felt guilty moaning about breaking his ankle.

Yes, he was bruised and broken but he was basically fit and healthy, whereas this child… 'How long have you been in hospital?'

'This time? Three weeks.'

'There have been other times?'

'I come in a lot. Sometimes my blood goes wrong.' Her tone was matter-of-fact and she reached out and stroked his cloak. 'The other kids thought it would be an actor or one of the doctors dressed up. You know, like Father Christmas. They always say it's Father Christmas but really it's just a fat man in a beard. They're not going to believe you're a real prince. Do you have proof?'

Caught off guard, Alessandro glanced at Tasha. 'Do I have proof?'

'Absolutely. I brought the proof with me and I have it right here.' Throwing the little girl a dazzling smile, Tasha reached into the bag on her shoulder and pulled out a scrapbook. 'Have a look at this. Here's Prince Alessandro at a royal function at the palace… And he…' she pointed '…he's opening a hospital. Just look at those crowds!' It seemed she'd thought of everything, and as she turned the pages for the child, Alessandro stared at the pictures of himself at various royal events.

Something shifted inside him. Somehow he'd

managed to hide his feelings in front of the cameras.

'Wow. Everyone wants to take your picture. Is this your horse?' The little girl pointed to a photograph of him playing polo, and Alessandro nodded.

'He's my favourite horse. His name is Achilles.'

'Do you wear a cloak when you ride him, like Prince Charming?'

'Er—no. I wear pretty standard stuff—breeches and boots.' He gave an apologetic smile and she beamed and took his hand.

'What happened to your leg?'

'I fell off my horse.'

'Ouch.' She peered at the cast. 'You need people to write on that. It's very clean. You need messages and pictures and stuff.'

'You're right, I do.'

'I can help you with that. Can I wheel my chair down the red carpet with you?'

Alessandro looked at the flimsy strip of red fabric and wondered if it would survive. 'Sure. Let's give it a go.'

Who would ever have thought he was so good with children?

Tasha watched as Alessandro handed another

little girl a pen so that she could draw a pony on his cast.

Here, in the relative privacy of the children's ward, she saw a different side of him. He was patient, natural, amusing and, most of all, interested.

She'd expected him to try and keep the encounter as short as possible. Instead, he'd settled down amongst the children in the playroom and seemed intent on giving them as much time as they wanted.

'It was generous of him to dress up and play the part.'

Tasha turned to see a young doctor watching her.

The woman smiled. 'I'm Dr Phillips. Megan Phillips.'

Tasha dragged her eyes from Alessandro and stood up quickly, hand outstretched. 'Hi. I'm Tasha O'Hara.'

'Yes, I know. You're Josh's sister.' Something in the way she said it drew Tasha's full attention.

'Josh mentioned you.' She noticed the other woman tense slightly. 'I told him I'd love to talk to you about working in NICU.'

'Oh—right.' Visibly flustered, Megan gave a brief smile. 'Well, I love it.' She went on to detail the pros and cons and Tasha stared at the other doctor, noticing the dark shadows under her eyes. *Shadows uncannily similar to the ones under Josh's eyes.*

With a woman's intuition, Tasha sensed that Megan and her brother were a great deal more than just colleagues. She wondered whether the beautiful, fragile-looking doctor was the woman causing Josh stress.

'Well—it's great to meet you, Megan. Thanks for the inside info.' She decided to do some digging. 'So, how long have you known Josh?'

'A while. We first met at university.' Megan avoided eye contact. 'Not that we hung out together or anything. Josh was Mr Cool—but you know that, being his sister.'

Tasha certainly knew Josh had broken a lot of hearts. She wondered whether Megan's had been one of them.

'If you were at university with Josh, then you must know Alessandro, too.'

Megan gave a brief nod of her head. 'I knew him by sight, that's all, because he was part of Josh's group. I didn't exactly move in their circle. I certainly didn't know he had such a way with children.' The insistent sound of a bleep had both women reaching into their pockets.

Tasha spread her hands in apology. 'It's you, not me—I can't get used to the fact I don't carry one any more.' And it felt strange, being in a hospital and not working.

'I'd better answer this—I slipped off the unit so that I could catch you.' Megan checked the number. 'I expect we'll bump into each other again soon. Maybe we could grab a coffee or something.'

'Yes. I'd like that.' Tasha watched the other woman hurry away from the ward and made up her mind that they were definitely going to meet again. There was something about Megan's pallor that tugged at her heartstrings.

She looked like someone who needed a friend.

Tasha turned back to Alessandro, to find him being swarmed over by children.

Remembering the bruising on his ribs, Tasha strolled over and gently lifted one over-eager toddler onto the cushions. 'Don't climb on the prince. You might damage him and then he won't be able to slay dragons.'

'She doesn't weigh anything.' His tone gruff, Alessandro rescued a little girl in a fairy costume who was about to tumble onto the floor. 'Who were you talking to? She looked familiar.'

'That's because you were all at university together.'

'Really?'

'That's Megan Phillips. Do you remember her?'

'Not the name, but I know the face from somewhere. Can't think where. I met a lot of people at university. Are you going to draw on my plaster?' Gently, he lowered the child onto the cushions and handed her a pink crayon. 'Go ahead.'

Tasha frowned. 'She knew you.'

'Without meaning to sound conceited, a lot of people know me.' He shifted his leg to give the children better access to his cast. 'It doesn't mean I know them.'

In other words, women always flocked to get close to him because of who he was.

'She knew straight away that I was Josh's sister,' Tasha mused, 'which means she must know Josh pretty well. I can't imagine he exactly spends his time waltzing around the hospital talking about me.'

'They work together. They probably chatted in the hospital restaurant over a stale chicken sandwich.'

'Prince Alessandro?' A small girl with her hair in bunches and wearing thick glasses squinted up at him. 'It's time for our story. Will you read it?'

Tasha watched as Alessandro smiled and scooped the child onto his lap.

He was a natural. And he possessed exactly the right combination of strength and warmth.

Strength.

Meeting his eyes, she stared at him for a long moment, wondering what would have happened had Josh not arrived when he had.

She and Alessandro would finally have slept together.

Tasha swallowed. She didn't know whether to feel regret or relief.

CHAPTER SEVEN

'REALLY, we should have invited the press. It would have been a perfect photo call. Even your mother would have approved.' Tasha kept her tone light but underneath she was shaken up. His gentleness with the children didn't fit with the image she had of him as an arrogant playboy.

'If I'd invited the press then I would have been accused of being manipulative.' Alessandro hobbled through to the kitchen, propped himself on one crutch and grabbed a cold beer from the fridge. 'I don't want to be in the newspapers at the expense of some poor family who is going through hell. Neither do I want an innocent child's private trauma broadcast to the world. I don't subscribe to the school of thought that we should all know everything about everyone.' He slammed the fridge door shut, snapped the top of the bottle and drank while Tasha stared at him in amazement.

'What's got into you?'

He lowered the bottle slowly. 'How do you do it?' His tone was savage. 'How do you go there day after day and work with those poor kids? Doesn't it break you apart, seeing them sick?'

She was stunned by the emotion in his voice. 'Yes, sometimes. It isn't always easy, but it's almost always rewarding. And the reason I go in there and work with those kids is because most of the time I make a difference. I'm not saying I can cure them all—' her own voice shook slightly '—but I do everything I can to make a horrid experience better. Some doctors think it's just about throwing the right treatment at a child, but they're wrong. *How* you treat the child is almost as important. Say the wrong thing and suddenly they're twice as scared and anxious.'

Alessandro drained his beer and thumped the empty bottle down on the shiny surface. 'I'm never complaining about my ankle again.'

'Actually, you haven't complained. Not once. Even when you've been in agony,' she muttered. 'You're brave.'

'Brave?' He gave a humourless laugh. 'Brave is that little girl who is never going to walk, or that boy who's on his tenth operation. They humble you, don't they? I mean...' he licked his lips '...we adults moan about the slightest thing. We moan about the weather, our workload, our family, but those kids—they're stuck in bed when they should be out playing with their friends and not even thinking about the way their bodies work, but they don't complain. They're smiling and getting on with it. That sweet little girl without the two front teeth—'

'Hattie?'

'Yeah—the one waiting for a transplant. Do you know that her mum travels two hundred miles to be with her—then she drives home when little Hattie's asleep so that she can spend some time with her two teenagers?' He dragged his hand through his hair and shook his head in disbelief. 'Then drives back again before Hattie wakes up in the morning. Can you imagine living like that?'

'Exhausting. Mentally and physically. Which is, I presume, why you offered her the use of your helicopter.' The generosity of the gesture still shocked her. 'I saw her mother crying and assumed she'd had bad news or something. Then she told me you'd promised to ferry her backwards and forwards until Hattie is discharged. She was completely overcome.'

'It was nothing.' He dismissed his contribution

with a frown. 'It will give my pilot something to do. Do you come across cases like that often?'

'When parents have to travel a long way? Yes. Especially in a rural area like this. And St Piran's is a specialist unit so I expect they take kids from a wide distance.'

Alessandro let out a long breath. 'How long until she gets her transplant?'

'I think they're exploring live donor. Her mother was telling me that a cousin might be a match. In the meantime she needs the dialysis to stay healthy.'

'She seemed so small and fragile.'

'Yes, well, that's probably because the kidneys play a role in the metabolism of growth hormone—chronic kidney disease can limit physical growth.' Tasha helped herself to an apple from the fruit bowl. 'Not that I know anything about Hattie's particular case, of course. I'm just talking generally.'

'If I throw money at it, can I make it go away?' His rough question brought a lump to her throat.

He cared.

'No. But you've already made it easier. She has her mum with her until she goes to sleep. That's a really big deal when you're eight.'

'You're wasted here, looking after me.' He

leaned his hips against the counter, his expression serious. 'You should get out there and use that training of yours.'

'Are you trying to get rid of me?'

'No, but I could see how skilled you were with those kids and I know that's what you should be doing. Have you lost your confidence? Is that what's going on here? This whole thing with that idiot you used to work for—has it shaken you up?'

Startled, she felt her breath catch. 'Maybe,' she croaked. 'Just a little.' It was better to tell herself that than believe that she was there because of him. 'I'm still afraid no one will want me. But I've started looking. There just aren't that many speciality doctor posts around right now.'

'What's your dream? Ultimately you want to be a consultant?'

'That's why I worked my butt off in medical school.'

'What about marriage?' His voice was gruff. 'Family? Kids? When you were seventeen that was what you wanted. You wanted the whole fairy-tale. What happened?'

'I grew up. The whole fairy-tale thing bombed.' She gave a careless shrug. 'Anyway, I always thought Cinderella should have picked up her own shoe instead of expecting someone else to pick it up after her. And who in their right mind is going to marry a man she met when she was asleep? If I'd been asleep for a hundred years, I'd want to get out there and party, not walk down the aisle with a stranger.' Tasha bit into the apple, horribly conscious of him. Even with broken ribs and his leg in a cast he was indecently sexy.

'Tell me about Hugo.'

She choked on the apple. 'How do you know about Hugo?' Looking at his face, she scowled and threw the apple into the bin uneaten. 'Josh, presumably.'

'What happened?'

'I don't know.' Irritated, embarrassed, she shrugged. 'The usual. I fell for a guy. He wasn't serious. Only that time I learned my lesson.'

'Which was?'

'A girl has to be in charge of her own happy-ever-after. And it doesn't always have to include a man. I discovered that having a career can be every bit as exciting as sex.'

There was a tense silence.

'If you believe that, maybe you've never had really good sex.'

Her heart doubled its rhythm. 'Or maybe I just have a really great career.'

'Maybe you do. But shouldn't it be possible to have both?'

'Maybe. But there are plenty of broken marriages in my business. Just look at Josh and Rebecca.'

'I don't want to talk about Josh.'

She felt his gaze right through her body. 'I think I'll just—'

'No.' Somehow he crossed the kitchen before she could move towards the door. 'Don't run off. Not this time.'

Tasha backed herself into the kitchen counter. 'Look, whatever you're going to say, I'm not—'

'I was going to say that you're beautiful.'

The words stole her breath. 'Oh. Well, in that case—'

'You were beautiful at seventeen but you were a child then…' His voice was husky. 'Now you're a woman.'

But she felt like a teenager, with her heart pounding and her breathing shallow. 'Sandro—'

'I want you, Tasha.' The words were thickened with emotion. 'But it's your choice. I'm not in a position to throw you over my shoulder and influence your decision. You can walk out of that door, or you can walk into my bedroom.'

Oh, dear God…

Slowly, her eyes lifted to his and her heart tumbled as she met the intimacy of his gaze. His eyes were dark pools of desire. And serious. There was no humour there. No mockery. He was an adult, making an adult decision, and he was asking her to do the same thing. She could walk away. *She could say this wasn't what she wanted.* Or she could…

'On second thoughts, forget the bedroom.' His mouth came down on hers and he kissed her. Desire punched hard and deep and Tasha slid her hands over his shoulders, feeling male muscle flex under her fingers as his mouth plundered hers with erotic purpose.

Dizzy, she remembered that Alessandro had always known how to kiss. It was obvious that the intervening years had done nothing but polish his performance.

Engulfed by sexual excitement, she felt his hand slide to her bottom, pulling her hard against him, and she tumbled blindly into a well of sensation.

Somehow—and afterwards she couldn't even remember how they'd done it—they made it to the bedroom, still kissing, and Tasha found herself on the bed, staring up into Alessandro's burning eyes.

'Do you know how long I've wanted to do this?'

'About as long as I've wanted you to do it.' There was no pretence between them. No shyness or coyness. And the sheer honesty of it took her breath away.

For a brief, intimate moment he looked down at her, and then he lowered his head and took her mouth again, tasting her, exploring her intimately. And she kissed him back with the same fevered hunger, taking everything he offered and more.

His hands made short work of her shirt and she felt the last two buttons ping onto the floor as he finally lost patience.

'I'll buy you another.'

'Don't bother.' Tasha matched his desperation, tearing at his shirt the way she had only that morning when Josh had interrupted them. It was choreographed madness as they stripped each other.

Naked, they rolled together and Alessandro gave a grunt of pain as her elbow encountered his bruised ribs.

'Sorry.' She braced herself on her hands, murmuring against his mouth. 'I'm really sorry. Just lie still and don't move. I'll do it all.' Before he could protest, she kissed her way down his body, her mouth infinitely gentle as she explored his bruises and moved lower.

This time his groan had nothing to do with pain. 'Tasha…'

She felt his hands slide into her hair but she didn't stop and then heard the change in his breathing as she explored him intimately.

Her intention had been to drive him wild but in the end she couldn't wait, and she slid up his body and straddled him, her hair tumbling forward onto his chest. 'Am I hurting you?'

'Yes—' his reply was thickened '—but not in the way you mean.' His hands gripped her hips and he shifted her over him, taking control despite her superior position.

Wildly excited, Tasha was about to move when he moaned something against her mouth.

'What?' She dragged her mouth from his and tried to focus on him. 'Sorry?'

'Condom.' He reached out a hand towards the drawer by the bed and she realised that the thought of contraception hadn't crossed her mind. 'We should—'

'Yeah.' *She was a doctor, for goodness' sake.* And it hadn't even crossed her mind. Fumbling in the drawer, she grabbed protection and then they were kissing again, hands and mouths frantic as they feasted on each other.

His hand was between her legs and Tasha felt the skilled stroke of his fingers as he drove her higher and higher.

'Sandro…' She panted his name—heard the growl of frustration deep in his throat, and then he was inside her and the sheer size and heat of him punched the breath from her body.

She came immediately, the explosion so intense and violent that she dug her fingers hard into his shoulders, holding on as everything collapsed around her. Dimly, through the burning fever of blind lust, she knew she should apologise for hurting him, but his hands were on her and he took her hard, each powerful thrust sending her spiralling up towards the peak she'd just left.

This time when she hit, she took him with her and she sobbed his name as he drove into her hard, bringing ecstasy tumbling down on both of them.

He lay on his back with his eyes closed, drained of energy. 'If I'd known it was going to be that good, I would have done it years ago and risked being beaten to a pulp by your brother.'

'So you're basically admitting you're a wimp.'

She lay sprawled next to him, one leg across his. Her fingers trailed over his abdomen. 'You have an incredible body, have I told you that?'

'As a matter of interest, which bit excites you the most? My broken ribs or the leg that's in plaster?'

'All of it. I love a vulnerable man.' Smiling, she pressed her lips to his chest. 'You're helpless.'

He captured both her wrists in one of his hands and anchored her hands above her head. 'Not that helpless, *tesoro*.' He rolled, ignoring the protest of his injured ribs. 'Do you know how long I've waited to get you naked?'

'About as long as I've waited for you to get me naked.' She stared up at him, her gaze mirroring the desire he felt. 'If I'd known you were that good at sex, I wouldn't have wasted the last couple of weeks tucking you into that bed on your own.'

'So we need to make up for lost time.' He lowered his mouth to hers, thinking that he'd never been with a woman who made him want to smile and ravish her at the same time.

'When the physio told you to take more exercise, I don't think this is what she had in mind.' With a smooth movement, she wrapped her legs around him and Alessandro hesitated, his hand locked in that glorious, tumbling hair.

'You do know I'm rubbish at relationships, don't you?'

'Me too.' She dragged his head down towards hers. 'Which is why we're going to make the most of this one while it lasts. Now shut up and kiss me.'

'Two skinny lattes, both with a double shot, please.' Tasha stifled a yawn as she dug her purse out of her bag and paid for the coffee. Glancing at her watch, she realised she'd had less than two hours of sleep the previous night.

'Any pastries with that?' The girl placed the coffee on the tray and Tasha looked longingly at the croissants and muffins, wondering whether carbs would wake her up or put her to sleep. Her brain too fuzzy to make a decision, she glanced over her shoulder towards Megan, who had bagged the only empty sofa in the coffee shop. 'Croissant or muffin?'

'Neither.' Megan recoiled and patted her flat stomach, but Tasha ignored her.

'I've got to have something or I'll pass out. I'll get a croissant and we can share.'

She wondered what Alessandro was doing.

Was he still with his advisers? *Was he thinking about her?*

'You look absolutely exhausted.' Megan's gaze was concerned as Tasha set the tray down and sank onto the sofa next to her. 'Aren't you sleeping?'

Tasha picked up the knife and sliced the croissant in two. 'Er—not that much.'

'Is Alessandro a demanding patient?'

Demanding? Tasha lifted her coffee and hoped her blush didn't give her away. Yes, he was demanding, and over the last two weeks he had driven her almost mad with his demands, but not in the way that Megan clearly meant. 'I'm just worried about the future. Don't know what to do about my job.' She told Megan the story, surprised by how easy it was to talk to her.

'Tasha, your job prospects are good.' Megan picked up her coffee. 'Between you and me, everyone knows that consultant you worked for is an idiot. Everyone is probably cheering you on.'

'Well, it would be nice to be cheered on from within a job.' Tasha nibbled her croissant. 'Still, at least Josh found me temporary employment. He's not bad, as brothers go.'

'He's an amazing doctor.' Megan spoke with real warmth and Tasha watched her over the rim of her cup, noticing the pink streaks on Megan's cheeks. Her brain slotted together the clues. She remembered Josh's reaction when he'd mentioned Megan's name and the way Megan's face had lit up when she'd talked about Josh on the ward.

'So…' Tasha kept her voice casual '…you know all my secrets. Tell me something about you. Are you married?'

It was the simplest explanation for her brother's behaviour. Why else would he be holding back?

'No.' Megan picked up her spoon. 'Not married. You know how it is with this job. It's hell on relationships.'

'That's true enough.' So if Megan wasn't married, what was the problem? Maybe Megan wasn't interested. 'Personally? I wouldn't have a relationship with another doctor. All those dinners in the bin.'

'I'd be fine with it. In fact, I think it makes it easier if you're both doctors—you both understand the issues.'

'Josh is terrible at remembering social engagements when he's working.'

'That's the person he is,' Megan breathed. 'He focuses on what's important.' She looked up and her eyes shone. 'He's a brilliant doctor.'

Knowing that she was looking at a woman in

love, Tasha felt a flash of delight, quickly followed by exasperation.

Josh and Megan were in love. No doubt about it. So why hadn't they got it together?

Was her brother letting his toxic relationship with Rebecca influence his future?

In which case she needed to give him a sisterly prod.

'I can't believe you've been back to the ward every day since the pirate party.' Josh refilled his wine glass as the setting sun sent a rosy glow over the living room. 'When you volunteered to help out with the prince-and-princess party I expected you to be there under sufferance for two hours and then leave, not go back for three weeks running!'

'Alessandro has appointed himself chief wish-fulfiller.' Tasha pushed the casserole towards her brother, careful not to look at Alessandro. She didn't dare look in case they gave themselves away. And she wasn't ready to tell Josh yet. He'd overreact and worry about her. He'd want to know what it all meant—where it was going. And the truth was, it wasn't going anywhere.

The relationship was intense and physical, but

she wasn't fooling herself that it was anything other than great sex.

'I never knew you were this domesticated.' Josh filled his plate a second time.

'Took me ages to make it so you might as well eat it. Today our prince arranged for some football player or other to come and spend some time with one of the boys. I have no idea who he was but he had a fit body. The nurses were as interested as little Toby.'

'Which football player?'

Alessandro mentioned a name that had Josh's eyebrows lifting in disbelief.

'You're kidding. How on earth did you persuade him to come?'

'He just picked up the phone,' Tasha said dryly. 'Alessandro is nothing if not persuasive. All those years of being in command, I suppose.'

Lounging in his chair at the far end of the table, Alessandro gave a dismissive shrug. 'I knew he was in the UK. It was nothing for him to spend a few hours with a sick child and it meant a lot to Toby. The little guy has been to hell and back lately.'

And Alessandro had been there every step of the way, giving whatever support he could.

Tasha felt her heart twist as she remembered

the look on Toby's face as his hero had strode onto the ward holding a football signed by all the members of the England team. 'How do you know all these footballers, anyway?'

'I know a lot of people.'

'Top athletes always know each other.' Josh cleared his plate. 'That was great, thanks.'

Top athletes? *Was Alessandro a top athlete?*

She knew he played polo, but as it wasn't a game she knew anything about, she had no way of knowing whether he was any good or not. Somewhere in the recesses of her mind she had a vague recollection of Josh once telling her that Alessandro could be the best if he put his mind to it, but at the time she hadn't really paid much attention.

As the two men talked about sport, Tasha thought about the time they had spent together this past month. Alessandro had proved a real hit on the children's ward and had spent hours with the children, talking to them and finding out what they enjoyed most and what their dreams were. Then he'd proceeded to try and make each and every dream come true.

'Megan Phillips thinks he's a hero.' Dropping the name casually into the conversation, Tasha poured herself a glass of water. 'He distracted a child for her yesterday while she took bloods.'

Josh's expression altered. 'You've met Megan?'

'Well, of course. She popped down to the unit on that first day to chat to me and we've got together since then. We went for a coffee together a week ago. She's lovely. The sort of woman you're instantly friends with, even though you've only just met each other.'

Josh put his fork down slowly. 'You went for a coffee? You chatted?'

'Er…yes. Generally when we women go for a coffee we don't sit in silence. Neither do we discuss sporting results.' Tasha gave the two of them a meaningful smile. 'Women know how to talk properly.'

Her brother was very still. 'What, exactly, did you talk about "properly"?'

'Oh, this and that. I don't remember the specifics.' She kept her answer intentionally vague, but the look on her brother's face confirmed what she'd suspected from the moment she'd met Megan Phillips—that there was something going on between Josh and the beautiful paediatrician. 'She really likes you.'

Alessandro sucked in a breath. 'Of course. *That's* where I know her from! It's been driving me mad.' He sat forward and thumped his glass down on the table, a triumphant gleam in his eyes. 'Megan was the one you spent the night with at that party when we were at university! New Year's Eve—that's it! We were celebrating because you were the new hotshot of the emergency department and my team had just won a trophy. You spent the night flirting with this gorgeous girl in a red dress.'

Tasha held her breath.

A tense silence settled across the room. 'I flirted with a lot of women. I don't remember.'

Alessandro smiled, man to man. 'You mean you don't want to remember. Your ego took a real bashing that night. Normally all you had to do was stand there and fight them off, but she wasn't interested. You had to work really hard for once in your life. It warmed my heart to see it.'

Tasha closed her eyes briefly. Why did men do this? Why was their form of communication either ribbing each other or punching each other?

Josh was still. 'I'm surprised you can remember, given that you had your hands full with that blonde from Radiography.'

Wishing she'd never prompted this conversation, Tasha pushed her plate away.

'You were Mr Cool, who was never going to succumb to a woman.' Alessandro was still laughing. 'And then the next morning you looked dazed—Megan Phillips got to you in a way no woman had ever got to you before. And it scared the hell out of you. I saw her around for a few months and then she just vanished. And you couldn't find her. It was a mystery.'

'There was no mystery.' Josh stood up abruptly. 'Nice dinner, Tash. I need to go.'

'Wait.' Alessandro sounded puzzled. 'You look like hell. And she looks like hell, too. You've obviously got something serious going on. So why aren't you doing something about it?'

Josh arched an eyebrow. 'You're giving me advice on relationships?'

'I just don't see the problem.'

'No. You don't.'

'I'm the first to admit I'm rubbish at relationships. That's because I've never felt anything for a woman, whereas *you*—' he emphasised the word '—obviously really care for Megan, so just give in to it! Accept that it's over for you and get on with it.'

'Well, you're such a romantic pair,' Tasha pushed the words past her dry lips, wondering why Alessandro's frank admission that he'd never felt anything for a woman should make her feel this sick. She knew that, didn't she? *So why did hearing him say it hurt so much?* 'I can't imagine why an intelligent woman like Megan would look twice at either of you.' She stacked the plates noisily and then caught sight of her brother's white face and paused. Anxiety shot through her. *She'd never seen Josh like this.* And Josh was her priority right now. 'Alessandro's right, though,' she said gently. 'Why not just finally give in and admit how you feel about Megan? What's wrong with that?'

Alessandro leaned back in his chair. 'Yes, go on. Admit that Mr Cool has fallen hard. Why not?'

Josh curled his fingers over the back of the chair, his jaw clenched, his face an unhealthy grey colour. 'Because my wife is pregnant.' He looked at them then, his eyes blank and soulless. 'That's why not.'

CHAPTER EIGHT

ALESSANDRO woke suddenly and glanced at the clock. Four-thirty a.m.

Outside it was still dark and rain was lashing the windows.

Turning onto his side, he saw that he was on his own in the bed. And then he saw Tasha standing on the balcony, apparently oblivious to the weather as she stared across the beach.

With a frown, Alessandro eased himself out of bed and limped across to her. For the first time in weeks the movement didn't leave him in agony.

He was healing.

Soon the cast should be off and he could begin intensive physio. He'd no longer need a nurse, which was just as well because he knew that Tasha had short-listed at least three jobs and she'd told him that she intended to get her applications off shortly.

And he had some big decisions to make.

'What are you doing out here?' Screwing up

his face against the rain, he realised that she was wearing nothing but one of his shirts. 'It isn't exactly Mediterranean weather. Your climate sucks.'

She shrugged him off. 'Go back to bed, Alessandro.'

Hearing the ice in her tone, Alessandro stilled. Underneath the soaked shirt, her shoulders were stiff. 'Are you going to tell me what's wrong?'

For a moment he thought she wasn't going to answer and then she turned sharply, her hair swinging around her shoulders, her eyes fierce. 'Why the hell are we doing this? I mean—*what* are we doing?'

The question was so unexpected that for a moment he didn't answer.

Programmed to recognise trouble when he saw it, Alessandro chose to keep it light. 'Standing on a draughty balcony in a howling wind and a thunderous rainstorm. We'll probably catch pneumonia. I suggest you come back inside while there's still a chance we'll live.'

'I don't want to go back inside.' She turned away from him. 'Just go back to bed, Alessandro.'

The storm of emotion he sensed in her was greater than the one swirling around them.

'Tell me why you're upset.'

'Why would you even care? You've never felt anything for a woman in your life, remember?' She threw the remark back at him and he flinched.

'That was just banter with your brother.'

'No, it wasn't. It was the truth. You never *have* felt anything for a woman in your life. Why do men do that?' She reached up and pushed her sodden hair out of her eyes. 'I mean, what is so cool about staying single and not committing?'

Alessandro stilled. 'You tell me. You're single. And I haven't seen you making a commitment.'

Her eyes flew to his and then she turned away. 'Just ignore me. I don't know what's wrong—it's just this thing that's happening between Josh and Megan.'

He knew a lie when he heard one.

Josh had been right, Alessandro thought grimly, when he'd said that his sister wasn't capable of not becoming emotionally involved.

Gently, he closed his hands over her shoulders and turned her to face him. 'Tash, look at me.'

She glared at him fiercely and tried to pull out of his grip. 'Just go back to bed. I'll be fine.'

'We're going to talk about this.'

'No, we're not.'

'At least tell me if this is about us or Josh?'

'I'm worried about him.' She was rigid and tense and then the next moment she leaned against him and buried her face in his chest. 'I've never seen him like this. He's so big and tough. Nothing bothers him. There's nothing he can't handle. But tonight he looked really…defeated.'

Alessandro hesitated and then stroked his hand over her head. 'You're right that he's big and tough. He'll handle it.'

'The truth is, I don't think he's ever really been in love before. But with Megan—it's real, Sandro. He really loves her. And she really loves him. Did you see his face when he told us Rebecca is pregnant? What a mess. What a complete and utter mess. When two people love each other that much, they should be together, no matter what the obstacles.'

He wondered if she realised what she was saying.

Feeling cold, Alessandro folded his arms around her and held her close, ignoring the rain that trickled down the back of his neck. Through the thin fabric of his shirt, her body felt warm and soft. And vulnerable.

She might talk blithely about sex without commitment, but she wanted love to exist.

She wanted it badly.

He gave a shiver.

He'd kidded himself that their relationship could be superficial. That both of them could walk away. But Tasha didn't do superficial, did she? Whatever she said to the contrary, she wanted the whole fairy-tale, just as she had as an idealistic teenager. Maybe she didn't even realise it herself, but it was perfectly obvious to him.

'Don't worry about Josh. He'll sort it out.'

'How can he? The woman he's about to divorce is having his child and there's no way Josh would *ever* leave his child. Never. Not after what happened to us as kids.' She lifted her hands to her face and he realised that the raindrops were mingling with her tears.

'Don't cry.' For some reason her tears disturbed him more than the realisation that she hadn't changed. Tasha wasn't a crier. 'Damn it, Tash—don't cry.'

'Sorry.' Her voice was thickened as she scrubbed at her face with her hand, 'I'm really sorry, but I love my brother and I hate to see him in this situation. He should be with Megan but I know Josh will never divorce Rebecca now she's pregnant. And she knows that.' She sniffed. 'That's why she did it. I know Josh is to blame too, but why would any woman want to have a baby with a man who doesn't love her? And quite honestly I don't think she loves him either. She just likes the idea of being married to a doctor. I just don't get it.'

Cold spread through his body as he thought of his own parents. 'A loveless marriage isn't exactly a rare occurrence, *tesoro*. People marry for many different reasons.'

Like political convenience.

'But what about the child? When Dad left...' her breathing was jerky '...I thought it was all my fault. I assumed I'd done something. Parents splitting up, parents who don't want to be together—it's the pits. I know Josh will love that child, I know he will. But if he doesn't love Rebecca and she doesn't love him...' She looked up at him, her eyes swimming with anxiety. 'That can't be good, can it? My parents split up and look how screwed up I am. And yours stayed together and you're screwed up, too.'

Alessandro gave a humourless laugh. 'Thanks.'

'All right, maybe you're not screwed up exactly,

but you don't let yourself get close to a woman, which is sort of the same thing.'

'You and I have been pretty close lately.'

'Physically,' she mumbled. 'And we were thrown together by circumstances. I don't want to talk about us. I want to talk about Josh. I want to wave a magic wand.'

Alessandro smoothed her hair away from her face. 'Josh has to work this out, *tesoro*. You can't do it for him.'

'I want him to be with Megan.' Her voice was desperate. 'You say they met all those years ago and it was special—think of all the time they've already wasted. They should be together for ever.'

For ever.

The words chilled him to the bone more effectively than either the wind or the rain. Alessandro took her hand. 'Let's go back inside.'

Tasha stood under the shower, waiting for the hot needles of water to warm her numb skin. She hadn't realised how cold she'd become, standing on the terrace while the rain sheeted down. She was freezing.

And, as if that wasn't bad enough, she'd made a total fool of herself.

All that talk of love and happy-ever-afters. It was a wonder Alessandro hadn't freaked out and tossed her off the balcony.

She needed to redeem herself fast. Salvage her pride before it ended up in a disorderly heap like last time.

Turning off the shower, she wrapped herself in a warm towel and walked through to the bedroom.

Crossing her legs on the bed, she switched on her laptop, intending to continue her search for jobs. But the moment the search engine appeared on the screen, she found herself typing in *'Prince Alessandro of San Savarre'*.

Glancing quickly towards the door, she checked that Alessandro was still occupied making hot drinks in the kitchen, then clicked the search button.

'Great,' she muttered. 'Over six million results. What on earth is he doing with you, Tasha?'

But the answer to that was all too obvious. He was enjoying convenient sex while he was trapped in Cornwall. Soon he'd be back to his old life, playing polo and presiding over state occasions.

She ignored all the references to his role as

Crown Prince and instead clicked on a result that said 'Sporting Legend'.

As she read, she realised how little she knew him.

He was a top polo player. One of the best in the world, with the potential to be *the* best in the world.

Tasha scrolled down the other results.

The Prince of Polo.

Alessandro the Great.

As she scanned the articles, the same words were repeated over and over again—'exceptional', 'the best', 'generous'. No wonder his injuries had been so frustrating for him. He was an athlete at the top of his game.

Absently, she scrolled down and clicked on another article hinting at trouble at the palace—the Princess, his mother, had expressed her disapproval at her son's sporting endeavours and insisted that he spend more time at home on royal duties.

Frowning, she clicked on an image of him accepting a cup for his team. He looked bronzed and handsome, his eyes burning with the fire of achievement.

Everyone was in agreement that the wild prince of San Savarre had astonishing talent.

Talent that he wasn't allowed to use.

Clicking again, she stared at a picture of him at a charity ball, dressed in a black dinner jacket with a tall, slender blonde on his arm. This time the caption read, *'Prince or Playboy? Will Alessandro of San Savarre ever settle down?'*

Her stomach ached.

They looked perfect together.

Regal. The only thing that spoilt the picture was the expression on Alessandro's face. There was no missing the adoration in the woman's eyes but he looked bored and desperate, as if he'd rather be anywhere else.

I've never felt anything for a woman in my life.

Tasha stared at the image on the screen and then glanced at the name of the woman.

Miranda.

She relaxed slightly. Wasn't Miranda the woman who had been engaged to his brother?

Tasha cursed herself for even caring. She knew only too well what a heartbreaker he was, didn't she? No woman held his attention for more than five minutes. It probably didn't help that he'd been fed a diet of female adoration from his cradle.

He wanted her now, but she didn't fool herself that he would want her once the cast was off his leg and they were no longer trapped together in this small, safe world they'd created.

Panic rushed through her.

She wasn't going to do that again. She wasn't going to jeopardise her career for a relationship.

Still fiddling, she followed another link and saw images of a car wreck.

Apart from his tension in her car the other day, his feelings about the accident were something he didn't reveal. And yet it had changed everything for him.

According to the report, his brother had been alone in the car the night of the crash.

Tasha was still puzzling over that when she heard his footsteps. Quickly she exited the site and deleted the search history. No way did she want him knowing she was looking him up. That would be beyond embarrassing and she'd already embarrassed herself enough with all that talk of love and soul mates.

'I made hot chocolate. I thought you needed warming up.' Alessandro hobbled up to her. 'Are you job-hunting again? I thought you already had interviews lined up.'

'I was just playing around. Thanks for the chocolate. How did you make it with one hand?'

'I can do a lot of things with one hand. Want me to show you?'

'Not right now.' Shaken by a flare of sexual awareness, she flipped the laptop shut and put it on the bed. 'I need to have a serious think about jobs. After all, you have your appointment at the hospital tomorrow and it's very likely that they'll take that cast off. You'll be fully mobile again soon. I need to find myself a job.'

'So you're still Tasha the career girl, then.'

'Absolutely. What else?'

'Out there on the balcony you seemed to be extolling the virtues of love and family.'

'Ugh—for goodness' sake, Alessandro, I'd had a drink! Several drinks, actually. I always get morose after a glass or two of wine.' She put her laptop on the floor and finished her hot chocolate. 'And anyway I was talking about love for Josh, not love for me.'

'Right.' The way he was looking at her said that he didn't believe her and she decided to shift the focus of the conversation.

'Can I ask you something?'

'Sure.'

'Why do you think your mother blames you for the accident? You weren't even in the car that night.'

He put his mug down slowly and for a moment she thought he wasn't going to answer. 'I should have been.' His tone was bitter. 'I should have been the one driving.'

'Why?'

'Because he'd been drinking.'

Tasha put her mug down slowly, realising that those words had great significance. 'You were there?'

'We were both at a fundraising ball. I told him that he was too drunk to drive but he didn't listen.' Alessandro's expression was bleak. 'Antonio never listened, but that probably wasn't all his fault. My brother was treated as the golden boy from the moment he was born. He was used to issuing commands, not receiving them.'

'So he ignored you. Why wasn't he being driven in a fancy bulletproof limo?'

'Because he wanted to visit a woman. And she wasn't the woman he was planning to marry.'

'And he was supposed to marry Miranda, right?'

A tension rippled through his powerful frame and Alessandro sent her a strange look. Tasha was still trying to interpret that look when he turned away.

'I should have stopped him. Taken the keys. Knocked him unconscious. Something.'

'Hold on a minute.' Tasha frowned for a moment and then sat down next to him. 'If he hadn't been sneaking off, or if he hadn't been drunk—are you saying that's why your mother blames you? Because you didn't stop him driving when he was drunk?'

'She's right to blame me.'

'No, sorry, but she isn't. Antonio made his own decisions and it sounds as if they were all bad ones.' Tasha was outraged. 'You can't be blamed for what he did.'

Alessandro lifted his head and looked at her, a faint smile playing around his mouth. 'Beautiful Tasha—one minute you're as gentle as a kitten and the next you're a tiger.'

'I just hate injustice, and if she's blaming you then that's unjust.' She sighed and took his hand. 'When someone dies, people look for someone to blame. It's part of the grieving process. They want an explanation—a reason. I see it all the time at the hospital. That doesn't mean anyone *is* to blame. And you're not, you know you're not.'

'Do I?'

Her hand tightened on his. 'Yes, you do. It's also normal to feel guilt. And that's what's happening to you. But lay out the facts, Sandro. Take away the emotion. Are you really to blame?'

There was a long silence and his hand closed over hers. 'Perhaps not.'

'Definitely not.'

'Tasha—about what you said on the balcony…'

'I was waffling. Take no notice of anything I say when I'm upset. And you're right—this is one thing Josh has to sort out by himself.' She deliberately chose to focus her attention on her brother's relationship rather than theirs. 'We should get some sleep. I'm surfing in the morning and you have that magazine interview.'

A faint frown touched his brows. 'You don't have to leave the house just because I have an interview.'

'Easier if they don't know about us.' Tasha slid into bed and flipped off the light. 'I'll go down to the beach as soon as it's light.'

'Tasha—'

'What?'

'I haven't told anyone about that before.'

She pulled up the covers. 'It wasn't your fault, Sandro. You weren't responsible. He was an adult and he made his own decision. You know it's true.'

He hauled her close. 'My ribs are healing.'

All of him was healing. Soon he wouldn't need her any more.

Once his cast was off and his mobility increased, he'd be able to cope alone.

She'd go back to paediatrics.

Back to her career.

And she was fine with that.

Absolutely fine.

'How does it feel?'

Alessandro moved his leg cautiously, aware that Tasha was watching him closely.

The answer was that it felt strange without the cast. It also felt strange to think that soon she'd be moving out. 'I feel surprisingly good considering I've had it in plaster for so long. The surgeon says that the bones are healing well but they want me to use the swimming pool as much as possible to build the muscle back up.'

And then he'd be returning home to San Savarre. No more delaying tactics.

It was time to face his future.

Distracted by that bleak prospect, it took him a few moments to realise that Tasha had asked him a question and was waiting for the answer. 'Sorry—I missed that. What did you say?'

'I asked if they're arranging for a physio to come to the house.'

'I told them I had you.'

Her gaze turned from concerned to exasperated. 'Sandro, I'm not a physio—'

'But you're a bright girl and you can talk to the physio. She'll do a session with us and then you can take it from there.' It was unsettling to acknowledge that his real reason for not accepting more help was that he didn't want anyone intruding on the little cocoon they'd created.

'Pool running is good.' Tasha whipped a notebook out of her bag and made a few notes. 'You wear a buoyancy aid and move through the water—I'll see if I can borrow the equipment.'

'You see what I mean? I don't need a bunch of different people traipsing through the house when I have you.'

She lifted her eyes from the notebook. 'So you're officially mending.'

'Apparently.'

Their eyes met and he knew what she was thinking because he was thinking the same thing. That this was the end.

They were both moving on.

As someone who did 'moving on' better than

most, Alessandro waited for the rush of relief that inevitably followed the demise of a relationship.

It didn't come.

'They're pleased with the rate of healing.' He maintained the conversation, even though his mind was elsewhere.

'So—that's that, then. You're not going to need a nurse for much longer.'

A nurse? No. He didn't need a nurse.

But that didn't mean—

Making a decision, Alessandro took a deep breath. 'There's something I need to say to you.'

'It's perfect timing.' Her smile was dazzling and she interrupted before he could say what he wanted to say. 'I have an interview on Friday. The job looks really interesting and apparently it's a very progressive department so they might even be able to cope with me.'

The news that she had an interview landed like a thud in his stomach. 'Tasha—'

'How honest do you think I should be about why I left my last job? My natural instinct is to tell the truth, but I have to admit that my natural instinct sometimes gets me into trouble— Oh!' Her flow of speech was cut off as Alessandro crushed his mouth down on hers.

Her lips were warm and sweet and what had

begun as a silencing exercise fast turned into a sensual feast. 'God, you taste fantastic.'

'Sandro…' She moaned his name and slid her arms around his neck. As the kiss heated up Alessandro found it hard to remember what he'd wanted to say.

'Wait.' He dragged his mouth from hers, trying to focus through the burn of raw lust that heated his body. 'We have to talk.' He felt the tension ripple through her and wondered why she would react like that when she didn't even know what he was going to ask.

'No, we don't. You don't need to say anything.' Eyes closed, she muttered the words against his mouth. 'We always knew this was just for now. You're moving on. I'm moving on. No worries— although I have to admit I'm going to miss the sex…'

Alessandro pulled his mouth from hers. Her words should have brought him nothing but relief. Instead, tension spread across his shoulders. 'I'm not ready to move on. That's what I'm trying to tell you.'

Her eyes opened slowly. 'You're not?'

'No.'

He stroked his thumbs over her cheeks, thinking that she had the most beautiful eyes he'd ever seen. 'At the weekend I have a high-profile wedding to attend. The Earl of Cornwall's daughter.'

'Is this in an official capacity?'

'Yes. And I want you to come.'

She stared at him for a long moment. 'Me?'

'Yes.'

'You want *me* to come?'

Alessandro stared at her in exasperation. 'Why are you repeating everything? Yes, I want you to come. What's so strange about that? We've spent the past six weeks together.'

'Oh—yes.' She cleared her throat and glanced around self-consciously, apparently only now realising that they could easily be overheard. 'So you're taking me for my medical abilities?'

'No. I'm taking you because I want to take you. I can't stand the formality of these occasions. I particularly hate weddings. I'd love your company.'

'But if it's an official appearance, shouldn't you be taking a princess with blonde hair and a haughty expression?'

'I'm taking you.'

Her eyes were wary. 'Am I expected to call you Your Highness in public?'

'No.'

'Are you going to be mobbed by adoring women?'

'It's a wedding,' he drawled, 'so hopefully not.'

She bit her lip and tilted her head to one side. 'So what would I have to wear?'

Alessandro smiled. If they'd reached the point where she was asking what to wear, it meant that she was definitely coming. 'It will be dressy. It's being held in a castle. Wear something glamorous.'

'A wedding in a castle?' Tasha pursed her lips but couldn't hold back the twinkle in her eyes. 'Sounds pretty downmarket. Might be boring.'

'It *will* be boring.' He sighed. 'All weddings are boring, so kill that shine in your eyes right now.'

'Are they madly in love? How did they meet? Was it romantic?'

'Tasha—'

'Sorry. Just asking. Good. Fine. Boring old wedding.' She gave a tiny shrug. 'I'll find something boring to wear, then.'

'I can't believe he's taking you to the Earl of Cornwall's wedding.' Megan gave a disbelieving laugh. 'That's...huge.'

'I'm the one who's huge compared to all those

breedy aristocrats.' Tasha stared down at herself in dismay. 'Can I lose a stone by Saturday?'

'You don't need to lose a stone. You look fantastic.' Excited, Megan hugged her. 'I'm so pleased for you. I know how much you like him.'

'I hear a "but" in your tone.' Tasha extracted herself. 'You think he's going to hurt me.'

'No.' Megan bit her lip. 'But any man as rich and gorgeous as him is bound to attract non-stop female attention. And he does have a reputation.'

'It's someone else's wedding, not ours,' Tasha said blithely, 'so his reputation isn't an issue.' Not for anything would she admit how she felt about him. Not even to Megan, who had become a real friend over the past few weeks.

The only subject they never discussed was Josh. Whenever her brother's name was mentioned, Megan instantly changed the subject.

'Well, he certainly isn't hiding you away. Every time I open a newspaper I see another article about that wedding. It's very high profile and by taking you he's making a statement about your relationship.'

Tasha felt her heart bump against her ribs. 'You think he's making a statement?'

'Of course. You've been living in this little

cocoon together, but now he's taking you out in public.'

'As his nurse.'

'Nurses don't usually wear glamorous dresses and have sex with their patients.'

Tasha choked. 'When I first met you, I thought you were dignified and delicate.'

'I'm practical,' Megan said dryly, grabbing Tasha by the arm. 'Come on. We're supposed to be finding you something to wear.' Without giving her the chance to argue, Megan dragged her towards St Piran's most exclusive boutique.

'You have to be kidding. I can't afford this place.' Tasha dug her heels in like a horse. 'I don't have a job, remember?' She'd told Megan everything that had happened at her last hospital and had been relieved when the other doctor had stoutly declared that she would have done the same thing in the same situation.

'Isn't he paying?' Megan paused in front of the heavy glass doors. 'Tasha, he's a prince. He's loaded and he's the one who invited you to this wedding. If he expects you to dress up in something glamorous and photogenic, he should pay.'

'He wanted to pay. I refused.'

'He offered to buy you an outfit and you refused? Are you mad?'

'No, I'm independent.' Tasha scowled at her. 'Do you know how many women fling themselves at him? Loads. And most of them just do it because he's a prince and rich and—well, you know. I don't want him ever to think our relationship has anything to do with who he is.'

Megan stared at her for a long moment. 'Tasha, he *is* a prince. You can't get away from that.'

'No, he's a man,' Tasha said firmly. 'These last few weeks—it's been so normal. He's just a regular guy. Well, maybe not a regular guy exactly because he's super good looking and devilishly charming and most of the regular guys I meet are complete no-hopers. But he doesn't act like a prince. To me he's just Sandro.'

Megan looked as though she wanted to say something else but in the end gave a brief smile and shook her head. 'Yes. Of course. I'm the last person to give advice to anyone on anything of a romantic nature.' It was the closest she'd ever come to admitting that her relationship with Josh was a disaster.

Tasha didn't even know if Megan was aware of Rebecca's pregnancy and she felt torn, knowing something about her brother that she couldn't share with her friend.

But she decided that it wasn't her place to say anything.

It was up to Josh to deal with it the way he believed was best.

Megan was smiling at her. 'I can completely understand why you want to buy your own dress and be independent. So let's do it.' Without giving Tasha a chance to argue, she pushed open the doors that led into the boutique, leaving Tasha no option but to follow.

Deciding that Megan wasn't as fragile as she looked, Tasha slunk in after her. 'I hate this sort of shop—they always look at you as though you have no right to be here.'

Megan lifted her head and smiled at the frosty-faced assistant. 'My friend is going to the wedding of the Earl of Cornwall's daughter. She needs something special. The photographs will be everywhere so it's a super opportunity to publicise the boutique.' She drew breath. 'Which is why you're going to give us a generous discount.'

Tasha cringed, but the sales assistant hurried over, as did her colleague.

'You are in absolutely the right place. We have several things that would be *perfect* for you.'

'Excellent.' Megan smiled. 'Let's get started. Tasha, go and take off those jeans.'

CHAPTER NINE

'SO THE Earl of Cornwall's daughter obviously doesn't believe in keeping a low profile.' Tasha blinked as another flashbulb exploded in her face. 'Whatever happened to quiet, intimate weddings?'

'Arabella describes herself as a socialite. She believes she has a duty to be seen.'

'Except that everyone here seems to want to see *you*.' Tasha flinched as a photographer leaned forward over the barriers and pointed his camera towards her. 'Whoa—unless you're airbrushing, that's too close. Please pull back to the next county. Remind me why I didn't specialise in plastic surgery rather than paediatrics?' She kept her tone light, but it was impossible not to feel self-conscious surrounded by an endless stream of beautiful women who seemed completely at home in front of the cameras. It was also impossible not to be aware that the crowd was chanting Alessandro's name.

'Is this why you were invited?' Hating herself for feeling daunted by the crowds, Tasha moved closer to his side. 'Does having you here get her more publicity?'

'Yes.'

'Don't you hate that?'

'Being the star attraction?' A sardonic smile touched his mouth. 'Of course not. Much more entertaining than being on the polo field.'

'Don't be sarcastic. This is exciting.' She slipped her hand into his and he looked down at her, his eyes glittering dark and dangerous.

'You look beautiful. If I throw you over my shoulder and take you behind the nearest large bush, what do you think will happen?'

Her stomach tumbled. 'I'll black your eye and the press will get some interesting photos. Forget it, Sandro. I'm all dressed up. I want to stay dressed up for a while at least. I want to enjoy the party.'

'Dr O'Hara—can you look this way? Can you tell us who your dress is by?' a photographer shouted across to them and Tasha froze.

'How do they know my name?'

'Arabella will have provided them with a guest list.'

'They want to know who my dress is by.'

He lifted his broad shoulders in a dismissive gesture. 'So tell them.'

Tasha leaned closer to him. 'I would if I knew,' she muttered. 'You're going to have to look in the back and see if there's a label or something.'

Alessandro looked at her in astonishment and then started to laugh. 'You don't know who designed your dress? Why did you buy it?'

'Because it's pretty and it looks nice on me. Why else?' Tasha glared at him, affronted. 'And I don't see what's so funny about that. Why are you laughing?'

'Because you, Dr O'Hara, are an original.' Cupping her face in his hands, he kissed her slowly and deliberately, ignoring the multiple flashes that lit the sky like a firework display. 'That's tomorrow's picture.'

'What? The back of my head? Now you've smudged my make-up,' Tasha grumbled, but her heart was racing as she saw the look in his eyes. Behind the flare of desire there was something else. Warmth. Intimacy. *Love?* 'I have a feeling that kiss is going to stimulate interest in more than the designer of my dress.'

'I have a feeling you could be right.'

Remembering the chill in his mother's voice,

Tasha shivered. 'Are people going to mind that you've brought me?'

He took her hand in a firm grip. 'I don't care what other people think. Come and meet the bride.'

The day passed in a haze. Tasha was introduced to what felt like a million people, but the only person she was aware of was Alessandro, who didn't leave her side. Whenever anyone called him for a photograph, he hauled her with him, as if they were surgically attached. He acted as if they were a couple.

Something shifted inside her.

Hope sprang through her natural defences.

If their relationship were just about sex, she wouldn't be here, would she? He wouldn't be holding her hand in full view of the wedding guests and smiling down at her with warmth in his eyes.

By choosing to bring her he was making a public declaration about their relationship.

Feeling ridiculously happy, Tasha floated through the ceremony and the speeches, barely hearing a word. Instead her brain was racing forward and she conjured a picture of herself in a wedding dress.

Princess Tasha.

In a dream, she greeted the guests eager to

be introduced to her, but her real focus was Alessandro, who looked spectacularly handsome in an Italian suit.

By late evening she'd grown so used to the sound of helicopters arriving and taking off that she barely glanced up when another arrived. It wasn't until she saw the change in body language of the guests that she looked over her shoulder to see who was attracting such attention.

Spying more suited security men, she glanced at Alessandro. 'Someone important?'

'You could say that,' he drawled. 'It's my mother.'

Tasha stilled as she watched the elegant woman move across the perfectly manicured lawn, flanked by security guards. 'Did you know she was coming?'

'Yes.' His tone was flat and Tasha stared at him in exasperation.

'And you didn't think it was worth mentioning?' Suddenly she felt grubby and self-conscious. 'If I'd known… I don't think your mother exactly approves of me—'

'Who I choose to spend time with is none of her business.' Still holding her hand tightly, he stepped forward as Princess Eleanor approached him. 'Mother.'

Mother.

Tasha winced. It was so formal.

'Alessandro.'

Still holding Tasha's hand firmly, Alessandro drew her forward. 'I'd like to introduce you to—'

'We'll talk indoors.' His mother's tone was colder than the champagne and she turned to the bride, who was almost swooning with delight that she had royalty in attendance at her wedding. 'Arabella. You look beautiful. Alessandro, I want to talk to you. Alone.'

'I want to talk to you, too. But Tasha comes with me.'

Without sparing Tasha a glance, his mother transferred her chilly gaze from his face to his leg. 'Do you still need a nurse?'

'She isn't here in her capacity as nurse.'

'I know why she's here, Alessandro. I'm not stupid. And neither is Miranda.' The woman spoke in a low voice that couldn't be heard by anyone around them, the gentle smile on her face giving no hints to the observer that the situation was anything but completely harmonious. 'And your little plan has worked, so there's no need to overplay your hand. Now, let's go inside so that we can work on damage limitation. Natasha, I'd like you to come too. I think it's best if you hear what I have to say.'

Tasha threw a bemused look at Alessandro but he was staring at his mother. His face might have been carved from marble. 'I agree. We'll go inside.' Without waiting for her agreement, he strode towards the wing of the castle that had been allocated for the use of guests.

'Ow—you're hurting me.' Tasha twisted her hand in his and he released his grip slightly.

'Sorry.'

'Look, maybe you should have this conversation with your mother without me there.'

'You need to be there.'

'Yes, she does.' They entered a wood-panelled library and two security men closed the doors so that they were alone. Princess Eleanor delicately removed her silk gloves. 'Natasha, isn't it? And you're his nurse.'

'Actually I'm a—'

'It doesn't matter. Did he tell you why he invited you here today?'

Tasha frowned, thinking that it was an obvious question. 'He needed to take someone to the wedding. This sort of event isn't much fun on your own.'

'Indeed.' The older woman's smile was chilly.

'But Alessandro doesn't attend these events to have "fun".' She spoke the word as if it were a disease. 'He attends because that's his job—to be seen. He's here to represent San Savarre. And the person by his side should also be representing San Savarre—'

'Tasha is my guest.' Alessandro interrupted in a cold, hard voice that made Tasha look towards him in astonishment. She'd never heard him use that tone before. He sounded...*regal*? Very much the one in charge. 'Unless you want me to walk out of that door and not look back, do *not* insult my guest. Tasha, would you give us a few moments, please? I've decided I do need to talk to my mother on my own.'

'Sure. No problem.' Feeling about as welcome as a virus in an operating theatre, Tasha made a rapid exit. The two stony-faced security men were standing guard outside the door and she slid past them and made her way to the ladies' room, hoping to avoid the inevitable gossip and speculation.

What did Alessandro need to discuss on his own?

And why was his mother looking so disapproving?

She was about to replenish her lipstick when

she heard female laughter outside the door. Anxious to avoid everyone, Tasha slipped into one of the cubicles and locked the door.

'I mean, he's utterly gorgeous,' a female voice said, 'so you can hardly blame him for not wanting to settle down.'

'He is gorgeous, but an utter bastard. Fancy bringing another girl to the wedding of the year.'

'You have to feel sorry for her. He's just using her to send his ex-girlfriend a message.'

Tasha opened her mouth. She wanted to alert them to the fact that she was there so that they'd stop talking, but no sound came out.

'It's a double blow to Miranda. First she loses Antonio and now Alessandro. I mean, he hasn't even ditched her for someone royal. Or even someone well connected. That girl he's with is just ordinary—like you or me.'

'Not like you or me.' Her friend gave a catty laugh. 'She didn't even know who designed her dress.'

'That's probably because it's the first time she's ever worn a designer dress.'

'And it will be the last. I'm sure he only brought her here to make a very public point to his mother. Judging from the bodyguards outside the library, they're having the conversation right now. What wouldn't I give to be a fly on the wall? Can I borrow your lip gloss? I left mine at that night-club last weekend.'

'Do you think she knows that he was supposed to be marrying Miranda?'

Tasha frowned. No, that wasn't right. Miranda had been his brother's fiancée.

'Little Miss Ordinary? Shouldn't think so. If she doesn't know her dress designer, she's hardly going to be up on palace politics, is she?'

'I thought it was common knowledge that everyone is waiting for an official announcement of the engagement between Alessandro and Miranda.' There was a pause. 'Does this shade look too red on me?'

'No, it's perfect. I heard she's been looking after him.'

'Oh, well, the poor thing is in for a rude awakening when she discovers what he's like. Still, this will probably still be the most exciting thing that ever happens in her life. She's just a nurse.'

Alessandro and Miranda?

Alessandro and Miranda?

Shaking all over, Tasha exited the cubicle. 'Actually, I'm a doctor,' she said, her voice robotic, 'but some of my best friends are nurses, so I'd be grateful if you didn't talk about them as if they're second-class citizens. Next time you fall off your horse, it may be one of them saving your life. And, just for the record, that shade is definitely too red for you. It's very ageing.' Without pausing, she swept out of the room, grateful that whoever had designed her dress had given her sufficient fabric with which to make a dignified exit.

He was supposed to be marrying Miranda. His brother's fiancée.

The tears lodged in a lump at the back of her throat, she continued to walk even when she heard Princess Eleanor calling her name.

'Natasha.'

Tasha thought about pretending she hadn't heard, but then turned, her expression blank. 'I'm just leaving, Your Highness.'

'I need to tell you a few things about Alessandro.'

'Actually, no, you don't. I'm the one who needs to tell you a few things about Alessandro.' As the last thread of her control snapped, Tasha's temper bubbled over. 'Do you know that he doesn't sleep at night because he blames himself for his brother's death? Do you know that he believes that you would have preferred him to be killed? He's

246 ST PIRAN'S: PRINCE ON THE CHILDREN'S WARD

living with that, and you're not doing anything to stop it.'

Shocked, the woman stared at her. 'Do you know to whom you're speaking?'

'Yes.' Tasha's lips tightened. 'I'm speaking to a woman who hasn't called her son once in the past six weeks except to nag him about official duties.'

'I have a responsibility towards my country.'

'You also have a responsibility towards your son.'

The other woman straightened her shoulders. 'You seem very concerned about Alessandro's well-being.'

'I'm a doctor,' Tasha said smoothly. 'I'm trained to deal with the physical and the psychological. And, by the way, that child playing over by the tree looks as though she has measles. You might want to remove her from all those people because she'll be infectious. Excuse me. I'm leaving now.' Wondering whether she was about to be arrested for insubordination, Tasha turned away, continuing her walk towards the exit.

Damn and double damn.

Her heart was hammering, her palms were damp and her hands were shaking.

She'd lost her temper again.

Wasn't she ever going to learn?

'Tasha! Tash!'

Hearing Alessandro's voice behind her, she quickened her pace. The last thing she wanted was to speak to him.

When a strong male hand closed over her shoulder, she shook him off. 'Let go of me.' Furious, she whirled around and faced him. 'You are an utter bastard and I hate you. I hope your bloody horse falls on your other leg and breaks it.'

He stared at her, stunned. 'You're upset about the way my mother spoke to you and I don't blame you, but—'

'I'm not upset with your mother. I'm upset with you for not telling me the truth.' Steaming mad, Tasha turned on him, eyes blazing. 'Why the hell didn't you mention Miranda to me? I knew she was engaged to your brother. Why didn't you mention that you'd taken over that role, too?'

His expression altered instantly and she suddenly felt like sobbing.

Instead, she punched him in his bruised ribs. 'Damn you, Sandro. I wanted you to deny it. I—I hate you.'

'You don't understand—'

'I understand perfectly. You were laid up in Cornwall so you thought you'd have some fun.

And that's fine, because I had fun too. But you didn't need to bring me here and use me to send some message to your girlfriend.' Her voice rose but she didn't care. 'You used me. If you wanted me to come to this wedding so that you could send your girlfriend some sort of message, you at least should have had the decency to tell me.'

A muscle flickered in his jaw. 'That isn't what I was doing.'

'Don't lie to me, Alessandro. I want to go home and I want to go home now.' Before she made even more of a fool of herself in public.

'Before you go, my mother would very much like to talk to you again. If you still want to go after that, I'll take you myself.'

'I don't want you to take me yourself. I'm perfectly capable of driving.' Snapping the words out, Tasha dragged her shoulder out of his grip. 'And I don't need to talk to your mother. Everything that needs to be said has been said.'

Suddenly she felt herself crumbling. 'Why did you bring me? It was cruel, Alessandro. Really cruel.'

He stood in perfect stillness. 'I wanted to see whether you would enjoy yourself.'

'Enjoy being mocked? Enjoy being ridiculed? I'm not that much of a masochist.' Her voice felt thick as she struggled to push the words past the tears. 'So now we've established that you should have brought someone else, I'd like to leave.'

Seeing a pack of journalists approach, Alessandro snapped his fingers and a sleek black car appeared from nowhere. 'Take Dr O'Hara back to my house. We'll talk later. In private. There are things I want to say to you.'

'Nothing I want to hear.' Tasha climbed into the back of the car, stumbling over the hem of her dress. The moment the car pulled away, she leaned forward and gave the driver a different address.

She had no intention of going back to Alessandro's house ever again.

It was over.

Josh rapped on the door of Megan's cottage. It had been weeks since he'd slept properly. Not since the morning he'd arrived home to find Rebecca waiting in the kitchen.

He'd been thinking about nothing but this moment—*trying to find another way.*

But there was only one way.

A seagull shrieked overhead and he could smell the sea. Normally he would have breathed deeply and enjoyed his surroundings, but there was nothing normal about today.

When Megan opened the door it took all his self-control not to drag her into his arms for one last time. 'Hi. I should have called, I know, but—'

'Come in.' She stood back and he saw hope flicker in her eyes.

It made it all the harder to step over the threshold because he knew he was going to kill that hope dead for ever.

Once before she'd trusted him with her heart and he'd broken it.

He was about to do the same again.

Blissfully unaware of what was coming, Megan walked in front of him to the kitchen. The house overlooked the beautiful sweep of Penhally Bay. He knew she'd had countless offers from developers. He also knew she'd never accept any of them. The house had been her grandmother's and for Megan the emotional ties were as powerful as the lure of the idyllic surroundings.

'Can I get you something to drink?'

'Just water. Thanks.'

'Water?' She gave a hesitant laugh. 'Josh the party animal drinking water?'

He ran his hand over the back of his neck, thinking of all the times he'd broken bad news to patients. It never came easily, but somehow he managed it. Because this was personal, it was almost impossible to form the words. 'We have to talk.'

'I agree.' Calm, she lifted a jug from the fridge and poured a glass of filtered water.

Josh watched as the water sloshed onto the side and then suddenly realised she wasn't as calm as she pretended to be.

'Do you want lemon? Ice?'

'For God's sake, Megan—' He prised the jug out of her hand even as he brought his mouth down on hers. He felt her gasp of shock and then she was kissing him back, her fingers curling tight into the front of his shirt as if she was afraid he was going to vanish.

It was crazy, insane, stupid, but he couldn't stop himself. His hands were buried in her hair and he was kissing her with a desperation that went bone deep. 'I love you.' He groaned the words against her mouth, 'I love you, sweetheart.'

'Oh, Josh…' Her voice broke and she made a sound somewhere between a sob and a laugh. 'I—'

'I love you so much, which is why this is the hardest thing I've ever had to do.' With supreme difficulty, he drew back, forcing himself to do what had to be done. 'That night we spent to-gether was incredible—'

'I know that, Josh.' Her voice was whisper-soft. 'I know, and—'

'No.' This time his voice was harsh, and he stepped back from her because he knew that if she stopped him now he'd never be able to say what needed to be said. 'You have to listen. You have to let me speak.'

Her eyes were startled. 'All right. Speak.'

'That night was so special. You have no idea.' He raked his fingers through his hair. 'When I left you that morning you were all I could think about.'

A tiny frown touched her forehead and she gave a bemused shake of her head. 'Josh, what on earth is wrong? You're making me nervous, I—I don't understand. Why shouldn't you love me? Why shouldn't I love you? I know it's been a bumpy road getting here, but—'

'I can't be in love with you.' He clenched his jaw as he saw her flinch.

'But—'

'Rebecca is pregnant.' His tone was raw and the words burned his chest. 'She's having a child.'

Megan stood very still. Behind them sunshine poured through the window but neither of them noticed. 'But…that's good, surely? It means she's moved on. She has another relationship.' Her voice faltered. 'Josh? Why are you looking at me like that? What's wrong?'

He couldn't remember ever crying. When his father had walked out he hadn't cried. Even that night Megan had been brought into A and E and he'd failed to save their baby, he hadn't managed to cry. But this time, for some reason, the obstruction in his throat was an immovable object.

'Megan…' He couldn't form the words. It was the hardest thing he'd ever had to say. *The hardest thing he'd ever had to do.* 'It's my child. Rebecca is having my baby.' He watched as the hope in her eyes turned dull. Watched as love drained away, leaving nothing but pools of pain.

'But—if that's true then it means…' Tears glistened in her eyes and she gave a sharp gasp and backed away from him. 'You told me the marriage was over. You told me—'

'It was.'

'But you were still having sex with her?' Her voice rose and she wrapped her arms around herself in a gesture of self-protection. 'We clearly have a very different idea about what constitutes "over". Oh, my God.' Agitated, she paced to the far side of the room and pressed her hands to her mouth. 'I would never have slept with you that night if I'd thought you were still together.'

'We weren't together.' Josh walked over to her but she whirled round, her eyes fierce.

'Don't touch me!' She backed away, the sob lodged in her throat. 'How *could* you? *How could you do that?* You were sleeping with me and your wife at the same time?'

'No!'

'She's pregnant, Josh.'

'It was just one night, weeks before you and I…' He sucked in a breath and spread his hands. 'I can't even explain it—'

'I suggest you don't even try.' The chill in her voice was agonising to hear.

'It was a mistake. Megan, she did it on purpose. She wanted a baby. This was her way of keeping us together.'

'You told me the marriage was over. You told me it was mutual.' The tears slid down her cheeks. 'But you had sex with her, Josh.' She was crying openly now. *'You had sex with her.'*

The memory brought a bitter taste to his mouth. 'It was just once.'

'Is that supposed to make it OK? Because I

can assure you it doesn't. It's not OK, Josh.' She scrubbed the tears from her cheeks with her hand and the frantic attempt to hide her distress was more disturbing than any accusation she could fling at him. 'You say you love me and then you tell me this? How do you think that makes me feel?'

Josh closed his eyes. 'Megan—'

'She can give you the one thing I can't give you.' Her voice cracked and she lifted her head to look at him, resignation in her eyes. 'She can give you a child and I can't compete with that.'

'I love you, Megan. And I'm telling you that because I don't want there to be any misunderstanding about what happened here. I truly love you, but no child of mine will grow up as I did, without a father. I won't do that. I have to make this work. For the child's sake.'

'Yes. Of course you do.' Her lips were stiff and her voice was a flat monotone. 'You're going to make it work, I know you will. You'll be a very happy family, you, Rebecca and the baby. If you don't mind, I'd like you to leave now.'

Josh opened his mouth to fight that request and then realised that she was holding herself together with difficulty. And so was he.

With one last look at her trembling frame, he turned and strode out of her cottage.

A happy family?

Not in this lifetime.

CHAPTER TEN

FURIOUSLY angry, Tasha stormed out of the car. It was dark, and the familiar smells and sounds of Penhally Bay should have soothed her throbbing head. Instead she just wanted to punch someone.

Remembering her manners, she leaned back into the car and thanked the driver.

'You've been brilliant,' she muttered, 'and thank you for taking me to the house to collect my stuff. Sorry about the ranting and raving during the journey. Just forget everything you heard me say.'

Alessandro's driver cleared his throat. 'Actually, it was quite a revelation. Usually His Highness's female friends depart crying. I keep tissues in my glove compartment.'

'Maybe you could add a shotgun.'

'Most women aren't like you, Dr O'Hara.' The man gave a regretful smile. 'Unfortunately. It's been a pleasure driving you these past few weeks.'

'Thanks, Mario. I just hope your bastard boss—sorry, I mean *His Royal Highness*—doesn't fire you for giving me a lift here.'

'No worries, Dr O'Hara. I'll get your cases from the boot.' Mario moved round the car but Tasha was already there.

'I've got it.' She hauled the cases out of the boot so violently that the driver took a step back.

'They're heavy—'

'You'd be amazed how much weight I can lift when I'm steaming mad.'

Alessandro had humiliated her publicly. Again. *She'd trusted him...*

Later she knew it was all going to hurt badly, but right now she was running on adrenaline in pure undiluted fury.

She took her surfboard from Mario and tucked it under her arm. 'Thanks.'

'Are you sure you'll be OK?' Concern in his eyes, he watched as she hitched the once-glamorous dress up around her waist. 'I'll just wait while you check your friend is in.'

'No need. I know she's in. I just texted her. Thanks for bringing me here and for being so kind.'

'You're welcome. You have my mobile number. If you need to go anywhere, call and I'll come and pick you up.' With a last concerned look at her face, he drove off and Tasha heard the door of the cottage open.

'Tash?' Megan stood in the doorway and Tasha turned and strode towards her, dragging her cases behind her.

'Thanks so much for letting me come here. I couldn't stay at Sandro's, and if I went to Josh's he just would have said I told you so, and then I would have given him a black eye. And to be honest—' She stopped in mid-rant as she saw the look on Megan's face. 'Oh, my God—what happened to you? You look—you're— *Megan*?'

Megan's eyes were red. 'I don't think you can stay, Tasha,' she said stiffly. 'This is so awkward, but—'

'This is about my brother, isn't it?' Scowling, Tasha yanked her cases through the door, breaking a wheel in the process. She leaned her surfboard against the wall of Megan's hall. 'You can say anything you like and I'm just going to nod and agree with you. He's the one who made me go and look after Alessandro. If it weren't for him, I wouldn't be in this mess.' She kicked the suitcase upright and slammed the door firmly behind them. 'Let's lock it and unplug the phones.'

'I don't need to unplug anything,' Megan said

wearily. 'Josh isn't coming back. It's over. He isn't going to come round ever again.'

'No wonder you hate him.'

'I don't, that's the trouble.' Megan's voice cracked and she cleared her throat quickly. 'I love him. I've only ever loved him. All my life. I know you probably can't imagine that, but it's true.'

Stunned by that confession, Tasha slipped her arms around her. 'Don't let him do this to you. No man is worth it. Not even my stupid big brother.'

'I wish I could feel as angry as you.' Megan blew her nose hard. 'I feel as though someone has gouged out my insides with a knife.'

Tasha winced. 'That's not good. I'll try and help you feel angry. It's easier. First you need to stop focusing on the reasons you love him and focus on the bad stuff.'

'I can't bear to think about that.' Megan pulled away. 'And I'm being so selfish. You must be devastated. Do you want to tell me the details?'

'I found out that the Crown Pig Alessandro is virtually engaged to some thin, blonde European princess called Miranda or some other stupid name. He doesn't want to marry her because he doesn't believe in marriage so he used me to send her a clear message that their relationship is over.

That's why he invited me to the wedding.' Tasha crashed around Megan's kitchen, helping herself to a bottle of wine from the rack. 'I'm so angry I need to break something, but I can't break anything in your house.'

'Go ahead. It's the least of my worries.'

Tasha glanced at her friend's red eyes. 'How long have you been crying?'

'You don't want to know. It's embarrassing.'

'You'll be dehydrated. You need to drink something.' Tasha popped the cork on the wine and filled two glasses to the brim.

Megan's laugh bordered on the hysterical. 'The usual cure for dehydration is water.'

Tasha gave an airy shrug and handed her a glass. 'This will do fine. It's liquid. Cheers.' She tilted her glass against Megan's, worried by how fragile and broken the other girl looked. 'Drink. To sisterhood. And the therapeutic properties of blazing anger.' *She wasn't going to think about her own pain. She was going to blast her way through it and keep busy.*

'He slept with his wife.' Despite her protests, Megan drank half the wine without pausing. 'She's pregnant. But I expect you already know that.'

Tasha stilled. Guilt shot through her. 'Look—'

'It wasn't your job to tell me. It was his.'

'I know it looks bad, and I'm not trying to defend my brother, but knowing Rebecca as I do I can tell you it was all her doing.'

'It couldn't have been *all* her doing, Tasha.'

'Well, that's true of course. He should have said no. But he's a weak, brainless man.'

'Josh is strong and clever.'

Tasha looked at her with exasperation. 'You're focusing on his qualities again.'

'Sorry. It's just—I really did think he loved me.'

Tasha sighed, wondering whether the truth would make the pain worse or better. 'He does love you. I know he loves you. And if it's any consolation, I'm sure Rebecca was lying in wait on the bed in a skimpy set of underwear or something. Slut.'

'They were married.'

'Their marriage has been over for a long time. She was playing games.' Realising that she was probably making things worse, Tasha picked up the wine and topped up Megan's glass. 'Let's just forget it. Your life is a mess and my life is a mess. You can be sad and I'll be angry. Whatever works. Do you have any chocolate in the house? That's good for either mood.'

'There's a large box of Belgian chocolates

given to me by grateful parents.' Her cheeks pale, Megan sipped the wine. 'Do you want them?'

'Urgently. We'll share the box.' Tasha tripped over the hem of her dress and cursed fluently. 'I just need to get a pair of jeans out of my suitcase. I'm going to break my neck if I stay in this.' And break her heart because the dress reminded her of Alessandro. She'd dressed with such hope, never once imagining that this would be the outcome. Because she'd been so careful not to dream, somehow the pain was all the more acute.

Anger, she reminded herself. *Anger was easier.*

Megan looked at the dress. 'We had such fun choosing that. I thought it was perfect.'

Tasha retrieved her suitcase and delved inside for a pair of jeans. 'It was a ridiculous amount of money for something I was only ever going to wear once. And now it's just a reminder of a completely terrible day. I'm going to give it to the charity shop.'

'Do you know the worst thing? When Josh came here today, I thought he was going to tell me he loved me. And he did. Two minutes before he told me his wife was pregnant.'

Still clutching the jeans, Tasha stared at Megan's ashen face and bloodshot eyes and wondered if she could have done something to make it easier. 'I don't know what to say. Right now I want to seriously hurt him.'

'I think he's already hurting.' Megan climbed onto a chair and lifted a box of chocolates from the top shelf of a cupboard. 'If I read this situation in a book, I'd think it was ridiculous. Why does life have to be so hard? Start eating. I'm just going to go and wash my face.'

Tasha stood, staring out across Penhally Bay, feeling numb and exhausted.

When the phone in her bag suddenly rang she scrambled to answer it, heart racing. When she saw that it was Josh, disappointment thudded through her.

She'd thought—

Her finger hovered over the answer button and then she heard Megan coming back down the stairs and she lifted her chin and switched her phone off.

'Which one of them was it?' Megan's voice was hard and Tasha shrugged and dropped the silent phone back into her pack.

'Doesn't matter.' She helped herself to a chocolate. 'Thanks.' She hesitated. 'What are you going to do, Megan?'

'You mean how am I going to carry on working at St Piran's with Josh there? How am I going to cope with seeing Rebecca pregnant?' Megan dropped onto the edge of the sofa, her fingers plucking at the edge of her cardigan. 'I don't know. I honestly don't know. And how about you? You're living with Alessandro.'

'Not any more. No way am I going back there. I collected my things on the way.' Tasha wriggled out of the dress and winced as the zip tore. 'Oh, dear. Good job I wouldn't have wanted to wear it again.'

'You can stay here as long as you like. It's been years since I had a flatmate.'

'Seriously? I can stay? I was sort of hoping you'd say that. Are you sure it wouldn't be an imposition? Just until I find a job.' She wondered how long it would take for the pain to fade. *Never again*, she vowed as she tugged on her comfortable jeans. She just wasn't going to do this again. She was rubbish at relationships.

'Stay as long as you like, although I suppose that might be awkward for Josh.'

'That's his problem, not mine.'

'But soon you'll be an aunty and…' Megan leaned back against the sofa and closed her eyes. 'God, what a mess. The awful thing is I haven't just lost him, I've lost you. How are we going to stay friends? It's going to be so awkward.'

'I'm used to awkward. You're talking to the girl who told her consultant to get a backbone.'

Megan gave a choked laugh. 'I was forgetting that. You're so gutsy.'

'It's not guts, it's an uncertain temper,' Tasha muttered gloomily. 'And while we're on that subject I probably ought to warn you that I might be arrested for treason. I yelled at Princess Eleanor. And then I punched Alessandro.'

'Oh, Tasha…' Megan started to laugh and Tasha found herself laughing too.

'Will you visit me in prison?'

'You've got to admit it's funny.' Still shaking with laughter, Megan wrapped her arms around her ribs. 'You spent all that time trying to help him heal and then you bruise him again. I'm so glad I met you. Where would we be without girl-friends?'

'We'd be stuck with men and then we'd go slowly mad.'

Megan sprang to her feet and reached for a DVD. 'Let's eat chocolate and watch back-to-back trashy movies.'

'Sounds good to me.'

Megan hugged the DVD to her chest and then turned to look at Tasha. 'I was pregnant once.'

Tasha spilled her wine over her jeans. 'Meg!

You can't just make confessions like that without warning.' Without taking her eyes off her friend, she put her wine glass on the carpet. 'Who was—? Oh, God, I'm soaking. Oh, never mind.' Ignoring her wet legs, she bit her lip. 'It was Josh's, wasn't it?'

Megan nodded. 'We had a one-night stand—years ago. He didn't know I was pregnant.'

'But—'

'I lost it. At twenty-three weeks.' Megan drew in a deep breath. 'It was Josh who saved my life. But he couldn't save our son. He was just too little—too sick.'

Tasha felt the tears spill down her cheeks. 'Oh, Meg, I—I'm so sorry. Josh never— I didn't know. I had no idea.'

'Josh only found out recently, although he'd suspected for a while. That morning you banged on the door of the on-call room—'

'You'd spent the night together.'

'I told him then. He overheard something.' Megan shook her head. 'It doesn't matter. It's all in the past now.'

'Is something like that ever in the past?'

'Maybe not. I still ask myself whether the whole thing was my fault.' Megan spoke quietly. 'When I found out I was pregnant I panicked. It wasn't what I wanted. Or at least it wasn't what I wanted right then—and nature took me literally.'

'No! You know that isn't what happened. It wasn't your fault.'

'I developed complications, and…' Megan breathed slowly '…now I can't have children. I'm infertile. I lost our son. So perhaps it's just as well for Josh that he's having this baby with Rebecca.'

'No.' Tasha hugged Megan. 'Josh wants to be with you, I know that.'

'Well, that's never going to happen.' With a sniff, Megan pulled away and fed the DVD into the player. 'You rang me in a state of misery and since you've arrived all I've done is moan. It's the wine. Never give me wine. And stop being so unselfish. Moan to me about Alessandro.'

But Tasha discovered she didn't want to moan, or even talk about what had happened with Alessandro. It was all too raw. And she felt so foolish. Foolish for believing that what they'd shared was real. 'I don't really want to talk. But I do have a question.'

'You want to know why Alessandro behaved like that?'

'No!' Affronted by the suggestion she wanted to talk about Alessandro, Tasha glared. 'I want to ask you if you happen to know who designed this dress I've just ruined. Everyone seems to think I ought to know.'

Tasha slept badly and awoke early to hear a rhythmic banging sound coming from Megan's kitchen.

With a groan she rolled onto her stomach and stuck her head under the pillow but the banging continued. 'What *is* she doing?' Giving up on sleep, Tasha slid out of the bed and padded barefoot downstairs.

Megan was in the kitchen, attacking a chicken fillet with a rolling pin. 'Good morning.' The rolling pin smashed into the meat again. 'Sleep well?'

'Er—not particularly.' Tasha winced as the sound resonated through her brain. 'Megan—'

'I'm preparing something for our supper.'

Tasha glanced at the clock. 'It's seven in the morning.'

'I'm pretending the chicken is Josh's head.'

'Ah. And is that helping?'

'I think it might be.' Megan gave the chicken an extra-hard thwack and the fillet split in two. 'Oh, dear.'

'It's OK. It will taste the same.' Her head throbbing, Tasha pushed her hair out of her eyes. 'If it's all right with you, I'm going surfing.'

'At this time of the morning? You'll have the beach to yourself.'

'That's the way I like it. Are you working today?'

'Fortunately not. I have two days off.'

Tasha saw that the scrubbed kitchen table was covered in pages from the internet. 'Australia?' She picked one up. 'You're going on holiday to Australia?'

'Not holiday, no.' Megan gave the chicken one more *thwack* for good measure. 'I'm looking at jobs. They need paediatricians, you know. We could both go.'

'To Australia?' Tasha started to laugh. 'I actually think that's a totally genius idea. Let's do it. Are there men in Australia?'

'Apparently, but it's a big country, so if we're really careful we should be able to avoid them.'

'Great. When I get back from surfing, we'll look at it together.'

Tasha thought about it all the way down to the beach and was still thinking about it as she walked onto the damp, cold sand. Just as Megan had predicted, the beach was empty. The wind blew her hair across her face and she heard the plaintive shriek of a seagull.

For a moment she felt a pang at the thought of leaving St Piran, but then she reminded herself that she wouldn't have been working in St Piran anyway. She would have had to go wherever the jobs took her. And that may as well be Australia. Maybe that far away, it wouldn't hurt so much. Presumably the antipodeans weren't remotely interested in a European principality so she was unlikely to be turning on the news and finding herself looking at pictures of Alessandro.

Trying to block it all out, Tasha plunged into the sea, feeling the cold bite through her wetsuit. Australia had some of the best surfing in the world. She could visit the Barrier Reef—maybe learn to dive.

Somehow try and forget about a certain tall, arrogant prince who had played a starring role in her dreams for far too long.

Ignoring the heavy ache in her chest, she paddled out and took up position just outside the breaking waves. Then she sat up, straddling her board as she stared out to sea, waiting for the right moment.

Could she grow to love Australia the way she loved Cornwall?

Her cheeks were wet and she realised that the sea water had mingled with the flow of her tears.

Furious with herself for crying, she turned the nose of the board to catch the oncoming wave, focusing on the sea and not her feelings. The surge of water lifted her and she paddled hard and then hopped up on the board. She dropped down the face of the wave, feeling the speed build, and she rode the water, arms outstretched, knees bent. As she angled along the face of the wave for that single moment there was nothing else in her mind but the rush of speed and the sheer exhilaration of being carried by the erupting swell of water.

She turned and paddled back into the waves, repeating the exercise until she was exhausted.

Wondering whether Megan had finished bashing the chicken, she finally lifted her board under her arm and walked across the cool sand towards the little path that led towards the cottage.

It was the car she noticed first. Long and black, with darkened glass. Bulletproof glass.

Alessandro stood against the car, watching her, four powerfully built bodyguards positioned at strategic positions around him.

They looked so incongruous in this beautiful, wild place that Tasha almost laughed. But she discovered that she couldn't.

As their eyes connected she felt her heart ache as the pain she'd locked away burst free.

Horrified to feel a lump in her throat, she turned her board, deliberately intending to head back out to sea, but his voice travelled across the sand.

'Tasha, wait.'

She closed her eyes, clenched her jaw and kept walking.

Last night she'd held it together and she was proud of the way she'd handled herself. No tears. No begging. Just anger and dignity. She didn't want to sully an otherwise perfect performance.

'Tasha.' He growled her name. 'If you walk away, I'll assume you're a coward.'

She stopped dead and anger shot through her like a live flame. Furious, she turned. 'Coward?' She stalked back to him, eyes blazing. 'You're calling me a coward? Sorry, but were you or were you not the one who invited me to the wedding for the express purpose of sending a message to your fiancée?'

'Miranda isn't, and never was, my fiancée.'

'*Almost* fiancée, then.'

'I would never have married her.'

'But she didn't know that, did she?' Tasha pinned a sweet smile on her face. 'So you thought you'd give her a stronger message. Using me as the messenger.'

'That wasn't what I was doing.'

'Oh, really? Then why did you take me?' She glared at him and he sucked in a breath and glanced over his shoulder towards his body-guards.

'Walk with me for a few minutes.'

'No way. What the hell are you doing here, Sandro?' The name spilled easily from her tongue and suddenly she was back in his bedroom, in the intimate world they'd created. And she knew from the sudden blaze of awareness in his eyes that his mind was in exactly the same place.

'I'm flying to San Savarre tonight.' Alessandro's expression was grim and serious. 'There's something I want to say to you before I leave.'

'I've said everything I want to say.'

'Fine. I'll do the talking.'

'How did you find me, anyway?'

'I asked my driver where he dropped you. How's Megan?'

'She's doing just fine,' Tasha said coldly, knowing that Alessandro might well speak to Josh. 'Now, just say whatever it is you want to say so that I can get on with my life and you can get back into your bulletproof car.'

'I came to apologise for last night.'

'And you needed bodyguards for that? Now who's the coward?'

Alessandro's mouth flickered at the corners. 'Walk with me.'

She lifted an eyebrow. 'Is that an order?'

'No, it's a request.'

Tasha hesitated and then shrugged. 'All right. If you're finally going to apologise, this I have to hear.' She put her board down on the path, horribly conscious of his powerful shoulders in the perfectly tailored suit. Dressed formally he looked remote and intimidating, nothing like the man she'd shared midnight picnics with after hot sex. 'Make it quick. Megan is expecting me back.'

'Why didn't you go back to my house?'

Tasha gave an incredulous laugh. 'Er—isn't it obvious? Excuse me, but this is a waste of time.' She turned away but he grabbed her wrist and dragged her close to him.

'I didn't take you to the wedding to make a point.' His voice was lethally soft. 'I took you because I wanted you with me. And because I wanted to see whether you enjoyed yourself at something like that. You're not like most of the women who attend that sort of thing.'

'Thanks for the reminder.' She felt his fingers hard on her wrist and tried to tug herself free. 'I studied for seven years in medical school and I'm still studying—but nowhere in my research have I ever found a benefit for memorising dress designers. I couldn't care less who made my stupid dress. So you were probably right to dump me.'

'I didn't dump you. You dumped me.'

'You made sure I dumped you.'

'No.' He hauled her against him. 'That's my life, Tasha. That's what I do. I go to weddings, I attend fundraising events, I open hospitals, I go on state visits.'

'Why are you telling me this?'

'Because if our relationship is going to work, you need to know what you're getting into.' He drew in a breath. 'I did take you to that wedding to make a point, but it wasn't the point you obviously thought I was making. It was nothing to do with Miranda or anyone else. It was to do with you and me. I wanted to show you my life. This last six weeks—it hasn't been real, Tasha. Yes, we spent time together, and it was special. But we were cocooned in our own little world. I wanted to know if you'd still want to be with me in the other world I inhabit.'

All the air had gone from her lungs. She felt

as though she was the one with the broken ribs. 'You—'

'I'm sorry if you felt humiliated.' He took her face in his hands, his eyes holding hers. 'That was never my intention. I know you're not interested in the whole designer-dress thing, that's one of the reasons I love you. But a huge part of my life is attending events. I needed to know that you wouldn't hate the life.'

Tasha felt dizzy. 'Whoa…' Her voice cracked. 'Rewind. Somewhere back there you said something I didn't quite catch.'

A smile touched his mouth. 'I said I love you. I've never said that to a woman before. Ever. Frankly, I never thought I would. But spending that time with you showed me I was wrong. I love you.'

The words had the effect of a drug. Tasha's head spun. She felt decidedly strange. 'If you… love me, why didn't you say something sooner?'

'Because love isn't enough. It isn't that simple. Not for me.' He pushed a strand of hair out of her eyes. 'I'm very aware that when you marry me, you'll have to take on all of it. Not just me, but the whole royal role. It's a lot to ask of anyone.'

'When I…?' Tasha blinked. 'Excuse me, but could you stop saying these completely shocking things with no warning? There's absolutely no way on this planet I'd marry you.'

His eyes held hers. 'Why not?'

'Well, because you're…' Flustered, she waved a hand vaguely. 'And I'm…' She pressed her fingers to her forehead. 'Just—give me a minute here. Yesterday your mother was looking at me as if I were a virus. Now you're suggesting marriage?'

'It may surprise you to learn that my mother is your biggest supporter.'

'You're right. It would surprise me. She turned me to ice with a single glance.'

'Yes, she's good at that. It's her way of keeping people at a distance. But you impressed her, Tash. You were tough. You stood your ground. And she likes the fact that you have your own career.' He gave a short laugh. 'And the fact that you have no idea who designed your dress.'

'Precisely. I have my own career.' Her heart was hammering. She didn't know whether she was feeling terror or excitement. 'I'm not giving that up for anyone.'

'I'm not asking you to. I wouldn't want you to. You're a very talented doctor. I've seen that in the time we've spent at the hospital. I've heard the way people talk about you. But we have hospitals in San Savarre. In the capital we have a brand-new hospital with state-of-the-art equipment. And consultants who are interested in being progressive.' He paused, a wicked gleam in his eye. 'We also have beaches. Incredible surfing. Endless sunshine.'

Seduced by the picture he painted, Tasha glared at him. 'That's not playing fair.'

'I don't want to play fair. I want you.'

Her breath lodged in her throat. 'Well, that's a shame because I hate you.'

'No, you don't. If you hated me you wouldn't have moved in and helped me. You wouldn't have stormed off last night. You stormed off because you love me and I hurt you. I upset you.' He drew breath. 'And I'm sorry. I should have come clean with you.'

'Yes, yes you should.' Tasha faltered. 'So—so you were seeing if I behaved myself at the wedding? You were thinking, Does she use the right knife and fork?'

'No. I was thinking, Could we do this together? Could we have this life?'

'I overheard some girls talking—'

He nodded. 'I thought you might have done. It happens, Tash. When you're a public figure everyone assumes they know everything there is to know about your private life. They think they know you. But they don't. But now I understand why you were so angry.'

'Sometimes I overreact,' Tasha muttered, her face pink. 'Just a little. When it's something I care passionately about.'

'That's all right with me. I'm happy to be someone you care passionately about.' He slipped his hand into his pocket and pulled out a small box. 'I would have followed you yesterday, but I needed to discuss it with my parents.'

'Discuss what?'

'The fact that I was going to ask you to marry me.' Sure and confident, Alessandro flipped open the box and extracted a glittering diamond ring. 'I can't go down on one knee because with this damn ankle I don't think I'd ever be able to get up again.'

Staring at the ring, Tasha lost the ability to breathe. 'Sandro—'

Without pausing, he took her hand and slid the ring onto her finger. 'I want you to marry me. I want you to be my wife and I want to live our lives together.'

'But—'

'For God's sake, Tash, just say yes, will you? For once in your life could you not argue with me?' He took her hands in his and his fingers were cool and strong. 'Princess Tasha. Josh told me you wrote that a few times on your textbooks.'

'That's two reasons I have to kill him when I next see him.'

'Don't do that. He's going to be my brother-in-law.' Alessandro drew her against him. 'I never thought I'd want to get married. I never thought I'd find a woman I wanted to spend the rest of my life with. And then I found you. Being with you feels…right. It always did, even when you were seventeen.'

Melting inside, Tasha lifted her face to his. 'Don't ever mess me around. If you step out of line, I'll hurt you.'

'But at least you'll be able to put me together again afterwards,' Alessandro drawled, smiling as he lowered his mouth to hers. 'I'll take my chances with you. I've always enjoyed dangerous sports.'

'Wait a minute.' She put her fingers against his mouth, delaying the kiss. 'You haven't told me about Miranda. She's the one everyone was talking about. Call me insecure, but I want to know about her.'

He hesitated and then pulled back slightly, his expression serious. 'Miranda was my brother's fiancée, as you know. We were good friends. I hated the way my brother treated her and for a while...' he shrugged '...other people thought it would be neat if we got together. And maybe she thought it, too. But it was never going to happen. She's always been like a sister to me, but I felt as though I owed her something. But I also knew that to go into a marriage without love was the wrong thing to do. You helped me see that.'

'Me?'

'It was the way I feel about you that made up my mind. So the other night I had a long chat with her. It was the most honest talk we've ever had. I told her about you and how I felt.'

'And now she wants to kill me.'

'She wants to meet you.' Smiling, he lowered his forehead to hers. 'You're going to like each other. She didn't really want to marry me any more than I wanted to marry her. We just gave each other support after Antonio died.'

'I yelled at your mother about that.'

'I know.' He gave a low laugh. 'Thanks to you, she and I also had the most honest conversation we've ever had. It cleared the air.'

'So I'm not going to be arrested for treason or whatever and thrown in your dungeons?'

'I might throw you in the dungeons if you don't give me an answer soon.'

Tasha placed her hand against his face and looked at him for a long time. What she saw in his eyes brought tears to her own and happiness burst free inside her. 'Yes,' she muttered. 'I'll marry you. Just don't expect me to call you Your Highness.'

His mouth came down on hers and they kissed until her heart was hammering and her brain was blurred.

Finally Alessandro lifted his head. 'Let's go somewhere more discreet before our most private moment is captured on film by some photographer with a long lens.'

'Wait...' Tasha hesitated, torn between what he was offering and loyalty to her friend. 'I honestly don't think I can leave right now. Megan is in a mess—she's thinking of going to Australia. Making a new life away from Josh and Rebecca.'

'She doesn't have to go that far to make a new life. We need paediatricians in San Savarre. She could rent out the cottage here and make a new life for herself in the Mediterranean.'

Tasha stared at him, touched by his generosity. 'But Josh is your friend. And my brother. Will it be awkward?'

'Josh loves Megan,' Alessandro said quietly. 'He's crushed with guilt. I think right now he'd support any idea that would stand a chance of making her happy. Why don't you invite her? It would be nice for you to have a friend there. She can have an apartment in the palace. I'm not saying it will be easy for her, but at least she won't have to worry about the basics.'

Smiling, Tasha held out her hand. 'I love you, Your Highness, have I told you that?'

'No, but from now on I expect you to do so on an hourly basis.' He lowered his mouth to hers. 'And that's a royal command.'

* * * * *

Mills & Boon® Large Print Medical

January

THE PLAYBOY OF HARLEY STREET	Anne Fraser
DOCTOR ON THE RED CARPET	Anne Fraser
JUST ONE LAST NIGHT…	Amy Andrews
SUDDENLY SINGLE SOPHIE	Leonie Knight
THE DOCTOR & THE RUNAWAY HEIRESS	Marion Lennox
THE SURGEON SHE NEVER FORGOT	Melanie Milburne

February

CAREER GIRL IN THE COUNTRY	Fiona Lowe
THE DOCTOR'S REASON TO STAY	Dianne Drake
WEDDING ON THE BABY WARD	Lucy Clark
SPECIAL CARE BABY MIRACLE	Lucy Clark
THE TORTURED REBEL	Alison Roberts
DATING DR DELICIOUS	Laura Iding

March

CORT MASON – DR DELECTABLE	Carol Marinelli
SURVIVAL GUIDE TO DATING YOUR BOSS	Fiona McArthur
RETURN OF THE MAVERICK	Sue MacKay
IT STARTED WITH A PREGNANCY	Scarlet Wilson
ITALIAN DOCTOR, NO STRINGS ATTACHED	Kate Hardy
MIRACLE TIMES TWO	Josie Metcalfe

Mills & Boon® Large Print Medical

April

BREAKING HER NO-DATES RULE	Emily Forbes
WAKING UP WITH DR OFF-LIMITS	Amy Andrews
TEMPTED BY DR DAISY	Caroline Anderson
THE FIANCÉE HE CAN'T FORGET	Caroline Anderson
A COTSWOLD CHRISTMAS BRIDE	Joanna Neil
ALL SHE WANTS FOR CHRISTMAS	Annie Claydon

May

THE CHILD WHO RESCUED CHRISTMAS	Jessica Matthews
FIREFIGHTER WITH A FROZEN HEART	Dianne Drake
MISTLETOE, MIDWIFE...MIRACLE BABY	Anne Fraser
HOW TO SAVE A MARRIAGE IN A MILLION	Leonie Knight
SWALLOWBROOK'S WINTER BRIDE	Abigail Gordon
DYNAMITE DOC OR CHRISTMAS DAD?	Marion Lennox

June

NEW DOC IN TOWN	Meredith Webber
ORPHAN UNDER THE CHRISTMAS TREE	Meredith Webber
THE NIGHT BEFORE CHRISTMAS	Alison Roberts
ONCE A GOOD GIRL...	Wendy S. Marcus
SURGEON IN A WEDDING DRESS	Sue MacKay
THE BOY WHO MADE THEM LOVE AGAIN	Scarlet Wilson